SERVICE CALL

Summer of Adventures 3

Alex Silver

CONTENTS

SYNOPSIS

Can a chance encounter lead to true love?

A one-night stand with the sexy plumber who saves me from a leaky toilet sounds more like the setup to a corny porno than the secret to a lasting romance. Still, I can't get Tate out of my head after he rocks my world. When he walks into my life again where I least expected to find him, it's got to mean something.

I never planned to fall in love with the first guy I met when I moved to a new city, but Tate might be the perfect boy for me. The only catch is that his past makes him wary of relationships. Can I earn his trust and prove that some things are worth taking a leap?

Service Call is a daddy kink M/M romance between Rory, a trans daddy who is new in town, and Tate, a dyslexic little who is used to guarding his heart after getting out of an unhealthy relationship with his ex. It's book three in the Summer of Adventures series and it includes age play/ABDL, caretaking, and tickling.

CHAPTER 1

Rory

My first glimpse of Vancouver makes something settle in my chest. This place suits me. Like coming home even from the first moment the highway dumps me out onto a busy residential street. The houses give way to businesses and then high rises when traffic takes me across the Granville Bridge into downtown.

It's my first time in the city and it's a shock to see how many green spaces there are here. Especially when I get to Stanley Park and discover what amounts to a forest on the beach at the edge of downtown. I end up going around a scenic loop when I drive past the turnoff to my short-term rental, and I'm not even upset about it.

Ahead of me, the green gives way to a wide bay framed by mountains. I've seen pictures of the city, but they don't do it justice. I can't wait to explore everything. But first, I need to get checked into my rental so that I can be up early for my first day at the new recording studio.

The fully furnished condo next to Stanley Park that my agent booked for me to use while I find more permanent housing in the city is swanky. It's right on the waterfront, too. Probably going to put a dent in my savings, but I got a nice advance on my next project, so I'll make it work.

Once I get the keys, find parking in the building's garage, and bring all my stuff up from my car, I decide to explore the area. I'm too wired to lounge around. My temporary home is close to the walking path around the park. I join the late afternoon foot traffic, taking in the scenic views and indulge in some people watching.

I still can't believe that out of all the applicants, I'm the one Pear Pictures and Eye-On Games picked to work on their newest joint enterprise. A feature-length cartoon based on a new video game about a ragtag group of superheroes. I've put in my time voicing bit roles over the years. Now my voice acting is my primary source of income, but it's still surreal to think that I'm the voice of Gust.

These two well-known studios chose me to voice an openly trans superhero with a leading role in their latest big-budget project. I'd never have believed it myself a few years ago. But that was back when I was still coming to grips with who I am. These days, I'm more settled. That's a funny thought, considering that I've just upended my entire life to move to a new city in a foreign country, but there it is.

In the brief time since I arrived, Vancouver already feels like it could be home. It's in the way a lesbian couple smiles and thanks me when I offer to take their picture with their daughter in front of a giant statue of a whale. My heart warms at seeing them openly walking hand in hand with their child.

I take comfort in walking past businesses that display pride decals near the doorways to advertise that all are welcome, even though Pride is still over a month away. And it's damn near euphoric to see a gay couple kissing on a park bench, the taller of the two men sporting brightly colored hair and a trans pride shirt. That could be me, though the pronoun pin on my shirt is a more subtle nod to my identity.

My heart squeezes, hoping someday I might find my ideal partner in this city, too. The dating pool was much smaller in rural Washington state, where I grew up. Small enough as a butch lesbian teenager before I realized I didn't have to go along with what society told me I should be. Smaller as a kinky trans gay man. Not that I've been back to revisit my rural roots as an adult. Los Angeles had more options, but I never made romance a priority.

Connecting with the local kink community here is on my priority list. It's something I wanted to do when I lived in LA, but exploring my kinks always came in second place to getting my career off the ground. I joined an online kink forum ages ago, but haven't found the courage to do more than lurk on the local boards since starting my transition shortly after uni.

I can do more now that I'm here. Break out of my boring vanilla dating rut and find friends and potential partners who share my interests. And my kinks.

Before the move, I researched and there are a few kink clubs in the city. Places I could go to learn more about the lifestyle and meet like-minded people. Or I could go to a munch to meet others who share my kinks in a casual setting. I've gone with friends before, but never near where I live. Never where I could actually make lasting friendships with others who share the lifestyle I crave.

The best relationship I've ever had was with Kel, my sweet kinky non-binary college girlfriend. In hindsight, I should have realized much sooner that I might be trans. I spent way too many late nights awake until the wee hours talking with Kel about her gender identity to be so clueless about my own identity well into my twenties. It took hearing a director describing my voice during an audition for me to realize the wave of nausea that swamped me at being described as 'too girly' came from not identifying as a girl. Kel always says she is the only one who gets to decide who she is, and she's right. That was the day I realized her words applied to me as well.

When we were together, Kel called me Mommy, and that was the most right I ever felt with a femme coded label. In theory, being a daddy can't be much different from being Kel's Mommy. But I'm still anxious as all hell about trying to find a little to spoil. What if I don't measure up? The mommy stereotype is a nurturing caretaker, whereas I had it in my head that daddies are supposed to be disciplinarians. That isn't me. Strict rules and punishments aren't my style. I want to nurture and indulge my little. That intersection of my gender and what I want in a relationship was a tangled knot of a mess to work through early in my transition.

There was a time when I thought wanting to be that kind of dom invalidated my gender identity. I spent years letting my assumptions hold me back from what I want in my personal life. I've since moved past those constraints; with Kel's help.

She and I are still friends. Our relationship ran its course when she moved out east for a job interning with a fashion designer after we graduated. Now she's got a design company of her own and a genderfluid mommy she is happily married to, but we keep in touch.

I've met Tamara and I can see why Kel is happy with them. I don't think I could ever completely walk out of Kel's life after everything we shared. She was the one who talked me through my identity crisis over trying to reconcile what I'd always referred to as maternal instincts with being a man. Kel reminded me that Tamara takes care of her just like I always did. Regardless of whether she's in her role as mommy or if he's Tam and being her daddy. Neither title dictates Tamara's gender, so neither does my desire to take care of a little. Paternal instincts are a thing, too. Or just plain parental instincts.

Now that I've had a few years to wrap my head around it and get used to the idea, that seems obvious. When I was just figuring myself out and accepting the idea that I could be trans, well, everything seemed overwhelming and huge. Kel and Tamara helped me navigate all those emotional moments. Mostly by holding my hand over video chat while I looked up what I needed to do to get to where I am now. They encouraged me through finding a gender affirming therapist, a doctor to prescribe hormones, and a job with insurance coverage for surgeries. Even with excellent coverage courtesy of my day job, I had to save up for the out-of-pocket costs.

My years of scrimping and saving and putting in long hours were worth it. I'm more than happy with the results of my transition. Even with all the medical leave and short-term disability I had to take during recovery, I'm happy with where my career has taken me, too. It all worked out better than I could have imagined when I took the plunge of moving from Seattle, where I met Kel, down to LA after graduating. And now that I've moved again, I'm hopeful that my future here in Vancouver might just hold the little of my dreams.

All that starry-eyed hope hits a bit of a speed bump when I get back to my swanky temporary apartment to find water running out of the bathroom. There's a shallow puddle trickling along the low pile carpeting of the short hallway that connects the living room to the bathroom and bedroom. So much for a relaxing evening before my first day at the recording studio.

With a heartfelt sigh, I call the property management company listed among my relocation paperwork and resign myself to having a long night handling this mess. At least the hall closet holds a plentiful supply of towels to sop up the spillage. I get most of the standing water taken care of while I wait for a plumber to fix the leak.

CHAPTER 2

Tate

I hate dealing with property management companies. They're so corporate. Which always means bureaucracy out the ass and reams of paperwork. Most of my regular clients know that I have my business partner, Luke, handle the written invoices and most of the admin side of running our business.

My ex, Gary, did everything in his power to talk me out of partnering with my step-brother when the time came to buy out my uncle upon his retirement. Working with family can be risky, but Luke is the perfect partner to handle that side of things, so I don't have to.

Luke is more than happy to handle the parts I prefer not to deal with. It's not that I can't read. I can if I have to. It's just a massive headache. And I mean that literally. Reading large blocks of text under stressful conditions gives me a headache. Keeping the dancing letters straight while I puzzle out their meaning also takes me longer than it should and I hate having to do it.

I've mostly gotten past my childhood embarrassment over my dyslexia and visual processing issues. There's no point being upset over the way I'm wired. That's energy better spent working out ways to pattern my life so that I don't need to rely on the written word. My friends know I prefer to avoid lengthy text messages, and that if I have to use them, it's with the aid of the accessibility features on my phone.

In moments like tonight's emergency call, I can't help

thinking I should just drop DHHI property management as a client. But they've been using our services since before Luke and I took over the business, and I hate turning away a paying client. Especially one of the few clients who pays a regular retainer for my services. Luke would not approve of that move from a financial standpoint. I'm still tempted. Then again, money has never been too much of an issue for me, despite being raised by a single mother.

Mom worked hard to make sure I never went without. And my NHL star sperm donor sent regular child support. Granted, he only did it as part of the deal he and my mom made to keep my existence hushed up in the media. He and his family aren't part of my life, and that's his choice. I don't have much interest in a relationship with someone who only saw me as a potential scandal. The money he sent us made sure Mom could make ends meet working for minimum wage as my uncle's receptionist. She juggled that with finishing her accounting degree and being a single parent. Mom is my hero.

After she got her feet on the ground financially, the child support meant I got to go to summer camps, attend the best schools, and my mom could afford to take the time off from work to get me diagnosed when my learning difficulties started. She advocated for me with my school and made sure I got the accommodations I needed to succeed. Without her unwavering support, I might not have graduated high school.

Mom wasn't happy when I first told her I wanted to pursue a trade and take over Uncle Frank's business. She called it squandering my education. Part of her anger was that she'd spent my entire life swallowing her pride by taking money from my father to give me the best start possible. That was a sacrifice she made to give me more opportunities, and I appreciate everything she does for me. But I was always happiest when my uncle took me along on his work calls and let me help him do basic repairs. So I stuck to my plans and built on the business

Unce Frank started.

It's not a glamorous job, but I thrive on working with my hands. There is something almost magical about knowing how to fix something that people rely on daily without a second thought until it isn't there. I've never regretted my career choices.

Well, almost never. I sort of regret that I have to fill out these ridiculous incident report forms tonight. The impatient property manager is refusing to give me access so I can do my job until I finish with all his paperwork. It's frustrating because the form is printed black on white. In tiny letters in one of those fonts with the fiddly little serifs that make them even harder for me to decipher.

When I reach the third paragraph, there are bold and italic words sprinkled in willy-nilly, and I give up. I sigh and just sign the form without reading it properly. That's a bad habit that might bite me in the ass someday, but it's Tuesday night and this emergency call is making me miss the bimonthly littles' night at Adventures. I always look forward to my limited opportunities to indulge in my kinks. The timing sucks.

If I hurry, I might make it to the club before everyone leaves. Even if I don't get to play for long, it would be nice to see my friends. The sooner I finish the forms, the sooner I can get this job behind me.

I pass the snippy manager one of the pre-filled emergency cost estimates that Luke and I worked out a while back. He'll send the adjusted invoice tomorrow, and the company will have the estimate for their records. We intentionally quote slightly higher cost ranges on the pre-filled forms so that our clients don't get a nasty surprise with the actual bill. Repairs are sometimes more complicated than expected, but we still look good when we come in under budget on the final invoice with Luke's system. Luke is full of those sorts of business life hacks.

Gary was dead wrong about going into business with family. Working with my step-brother is honestly the best business decision I could have made. Years later, it still makes me shudder to think how close I came to accepting his arguments that Daddy knew best. Daddy might know best about bedtime, but ever since things ended with Gary, I've kept a safe distance from the people I play with. I know better than to get so tangled up in a relationship that I let a partner control my professional life or try to drive a wedge between me and my family.

The building manager finally buzzes me up to the apartment having the issue. The elevator ride up to the fifth floor gives me enough time to check in with Luke and let him know I'm out on a call tonight. He'll know to expect the full call description for the invoice in his inbox tomorrow morning.

I dictate a quick text using my phone's speech-to-text, since I don't want to be rude to the tenant by being on the phone when I get to his door.

Tate: Hey Luke. Dealing with an emergency call out to Westside Towers. Invoice in the morning.

As usual when I send him work related messages, he replies right away. No surprise there, since the call to come here interrupted our nightly check-in conversation and I had to hang up on him to take it.

Luke: Sounds good. Sucks you're missing your playtime though *wink face*

The reminder that Luke knows about littles' night at my kink club is still weird. It's not like I think of him as anything but my brother these days. Even if we didn't become step-brothers until we were in our last year of high school. It's still jarring to realize how well matched we could have been in another life. One where our moms didn't get married, and we didn't spend the first year of being brothers pretending we hadn't sucked each other's dicks

11

at summer camp.

Luke used to go to a different club, but after it closed, he surprised me by joining my favorite club. Adventures is my haven. And it hasn't escaped my notice that Luke doesn't come to littles' nights even though I know he would like nothing more than to be someone's daddy. Littles' night is the only consistent time I get to cut loose and regress around people like me. So I've selfishly let him continue avoiding it to give me space I shouldn't need.

It's been almost a decade since there was anything sexual between us. I should be able to handle having him see me like that. As a carefree, joyful boy without thinking it will change anything. I don't want things to change. Luke is my brother in every way that matters and the last thing I want is for our compatible kinks to somehow rekindle our weirdly complicated, long-extinguished flame. So when he offered to give me space by avoiding the littles' nights since I had been a member at Adventures longer, I agreed to his proposal. No sense tempting fate. Still, since I can't make it tonight, one of us might as well have fun.

Tate: I doubt I'll get out of here any time soon. Why don't you hit up Adventures tonight in my place?

Tate: Get your little fix or relax with the other bigs.

I try to keep the message brief to avoid weird transcription errors, but Luke will get the gist, regardless. The elevator arrives on the fifth floor, so I hit send before I can chicken out and delete it. If I invite Luke into the daddy kink part of my life, even just by playing in the same space, we might see each other in a different light. But he's my brother and I want him to be happy. Since being a daddy makes him happy, letting him stay away from his optimal dating pool is something I need to get over.

Besides, it will thrill my friends to have a new daddy to play with. Monty especially, if the way my best friend eye fucks my brother when we're at the club and he thinks I'm not paying attention is anything to go by. I tuck away my phone, hoist up my tools and go to knock on number five-oh-six.

I'm expecting one of the usual corporate types to be waiting impatiently on the other side. A brusque businessperson in a suit with their nose in the air and an awful attitude about anything that so much as mildly inconveniences them. In short, someone who is ready and willing to take out their crappy night on anyone unfortunate enough to cross their path. The sort of person who looks down on me for my work until they need me.

That is not at all what I get. The tenant gives me a grateful smile as they hold the door wide open. They glance between my coveralls and my tools, then bat their—no, his, there's a pronoun pin on his shirt—eyes at me.

"Hi, I'm Rory, he/him. Are you here to clean out my pipes?" Rory asks, then shifts anxiously as he realizes how that could be interpreted. Or else he had a sudden change of heart about outing himself with the flirty one-liner. "I, uh, didn't mean that how it sounded. Just need you to plug up my hole." He cringes. "I mean, my leaky pipe. In the bathroom."

This guy needs to quit while he's ahead, but I've heard it all before, so I just give him a knowing smirk. It doesn't hurt that he's looking sexy in the low-slung lounge pants that make it clear the man is packing. Shit, I try not to stare at his bulge. But if the distinct outline of his dick is anything to judge by, I'll gladly take him up on any cheesy innuendos he is offering. His tight shirt shows off a well-sculpted chest. Yeah, I might not mind missing my evening plans if it means I get to flirt with this guy all evening.

A handsome guy tripping over his tongue for me is a nice ego boost, even if it doesn't go anywhere. No guarantee he bats for my team, but he started the flirting and offered his pronouns, so it seems like a safe enough bet to reciprocate. "Yep." I nod. "I'm the plumber on call. Tate, he/him, at your service for all your pipe laying needs." I wink for good measure.

Rory gawps at my return flirtation for a moment, and I worry I might have overstepped, despite his initial friendliness. He rubs at the back of his neck self-consciously. The hem of his shirt rides up to expose a narrow strip of his soft hairy stomach. Okay, so the man has defined pecs, shoulders I want to lick, and a bit of a dad bod around the middle. Which I can totally dig. I can picture gripping those solid shoulders while I ride his dick, my own erection rubbing a trail of pre-cum along his round belly.

"Um, right. It's in here. I have no idea what a rim job has to do with a caulk gun, but the internet tells me it will fix my o-ring issues?" Rory turns to gesture at the interior of the apartment, which makes it easier to hide my amusement at the cheesy lines he's spewing.

I follow him inside, but I can't help making one more wisecrack. "Lucky for you, I know how to use my equipment." I heft my toolbox, but let my eyes say I meant something entirely different when Rory turns to face me in the washroom doorway. "And I'm proficient in both wielding caulk and rimming."

Rory returns my heated gaze. "Maybe I should watch you work your magic, then." He sweeps his arm toward the cozy little washroom where I can see right away that whoever installed the toilet did a shit job, pun intended. This is almost definitely a case of a cracked wax ring from before Uncle Frank took the contract with this management company.

My deeper concern is how long the seal has been compromised. Or more to the point, how much structural damage might lurk under the high end finishes that give this place a luxe veneer over all the cut corners. The soggy towels heaped in the hamper beside the sink appear to have sopped up the water that spilled across the floor. It might behoove the property manager to have me in to look at the other toilets to prevent similar incidents. None of that is Rory's problem, but it will end up going in my report when I'm done here.

"Sure thing, you wouldn't be the first to say I've got magic hands; I'm pretty good in tight places." I let my gaze drift toward his ass just as he turns to lean against the vanity, so he catches me checking him out. Moment of truth, hopefully I didn't misjudge his receptiveness to flirting with a man. I might have inherited my pro-hockey player bio dad's imposing build, but I'm no fighter if he takes a swing at me.

"In your line of work, I just bet you're not afraid of getting a little dirty, either." Rory's lips quirk into a grin. "Show me what you've got."

"Right, let's look at what we're dealing with." I brush past him and squat beside the toilet. Rory at least turned off the water supply to the tank, so the mess appears contained with the unit's hotel style white towels for the moment. Good.

I glance up at him and catch him staring at my assets. We exchange smiles with a little extra eye contact, unspoken attraction passing between us. If I'm not mistaken, he'd be up for a quickie once I finish the job. Totally unprofessional, except Rory isn't the one paying me and since it's an after hours call, it's not like I'd be on the clock when I finish fixing his toilet. Yeah, apparently I'm so hard up I can justify anything tonight. Or I can blame the zing of attraction straight to my balls when I look at him. Nothing wrong with two consenting adults acting on a mutual attraction.

He's hot. Crouching and gazing up at him while he stands nearby watching over my every move tugs on the part of me that is most at home when I'm playing at a daddy's feet. I haven't had anyone like that for more than a scene or two in ages. Too bad this isn't a scene. It's my job. Right. I turn back to the task at hand and get to work.

I flush away most of the water and add LiquiLock to solidify what's left. No sense making a bigger puddle than I have to. Should be a routine fix and I'll be on my way soon.

Except, of course, Luke messages me back and I forgot to silence the accessibility feature that auto-reads my texts to me.

"New message from Luke," the monotone voice of the virtual assistant announces from my pocket. Impeccable timing, the message arrives at the exact instant I get my hands covered in the slimy mess from prying the toilet fixture loose and scraping away the remnants of the old ring. "Do you want me to read it to you?" The voice chirps.

"Not right now." I grunt.

"Okay." Of course the AI takes that as a yes. Darn it all to hell. "Reading new message from Luke: 'Are you sure my being there wouldn't be stepping on your toes, Tater-Tot? I wouldn't want to intrude on your relaxation time.' End of message. Would you like to send a reply?"

I suppress a groan and resist the urge to check how much of that message Rory might understand. Hopefully, none of it. Why would he? Luke knows I use text-to-talk, so he is discreet when he messages me. Rory doesn't visibly react to the message. "Yes, text Luke: 'It's fine, have fun tonight.'"

"Texting Luke: 'It's fine. Have bun tonight.' Is that correct?"

I sigh, decide that it's close enough and Luke might get a kick out of my phone all but telling him to get some ass. "Yes, send." I agree. The virtual assistant sends the text with a whoosh sound effect. I can't resist glancing up at Rory to assess what he thinks of me taking a personal message while I work. "Sorry about that. I had to change some plans with my brother." I give him an apologetic shrug.

Rory brushes it off. "Don't worry about it. Doesn't seem to stop you from doing your job." He gestures as I continue to wipe the toilet fixture clean. He's right, I can multitask with the best of them and this is a routine fix.

"Yeah. We belong to the same club. So, you know…" I trail off as I pry up the last stubborn bit of wax from the old seal. "He's going to a meeting without me tonight."

"Ah, sorry to make you miss out, then." Rory leans back against the narrow vanity, watching as I fit the new wax seal into place.

"Not your fault. Shit happens." I shrug off his apology. "Someone's got to make sure the porcelain throne is working for you when it does. There, that should do it, now to reinstall the toilet."

I hurry through the rest of the routine install. The toilet is heavy and I don't want to risk cracking the ceramic, so I take my time with that part, but otherwise I could do this in my sleep. I've got more interesting matters on my mind. I might not be getting any playtime tonight, but I can at least scratch a different itch. Sex with the hottie who has been all but eye-fucking me since I walked through his door sounds amazing. Rory is sexy, and he seems into me, so why the hell not?

Once I clean up and put away my tools, I'm off the clock. I arrange my equipment by the front door. When I turn to face Rory, he's right behind me. His eyes must have stayed glued to my ass while I walked because I catch him ogling my groin. His gaze darts back up to my face and his expression turns sheepish at being caught checking me out.

I wink and let my eyes rove up and down his body again, appreciating the view. That bulge is just as promising as it looked at first glance. Either he is well endowed or he's at least halfway hard for me already in those baggy gray sweats. I make eye contact with Rory, licking my lips in anticipation.

I almost never hook up at Adventures. Or with anyone in the scene, but I still enjoy sex. Monty and my other friends all assume it's because I don't enjoy dirty play when I'm little. That's not the reason. The problem is that when I mix sex and being taken care of, it's way too easy to fall for the other party, hard and fast. Case in point, Gary. He had me moved into his place and following his rules in less than a month.

I can do a scene without it developing into more than a deep friendship and I can do casual sex with no strings. But it seems like the minute both of my deepest desires are being met by the same person, my heart gets involved. That's not something I want to deal with when there are only so many bigs to play with on the regular. More often than not, I opt for age play over hook ups when I have free time to socialize. But it's too late to go home, clean up, and get to Adventures to hang out with my friends. So if I can't be little tonight, I can at least share some orgasms with a hot guy I'll probably never see again.

"So, I'm all set here, want me to head out or…" I trail off, lifting my eyebrows suggestively.

"Or stay. Definitely stay." Rory steps closer to me, and I smile as he leans in for a kiss. The eager warmth of our mouths meeting has me rock-hard in moments. I reach for him, enjoying the firm grip of his hands on my biceps as we kiss.

He tugs me closer, but as much as I'd love to have him pressed up against me, I'm still in my work coveralls. I step back. "Just a sec. Let me take off the nasty coveralls first."

"You can take it all off. I've got all night." Rory eyes my crotch again.

"Yeah? In that case, mind if I grab a shower, too?" I take him at his word, kicking off my boots before I strip out of my coveralls. Not wasting time, I leave them draped over my work boots and tools near the front door. Rory licks his lips at the sight of me in my underwear and not much else. Good to know he still likes what he sees.

Rory chuckles self-consciously when he notices that I'm watching him watch me. "Sure. I imagine if I spent all day elbow-deep in other people's pipes, a shower would be the first thing on my mind too, huh?"

"Pretty much. That, and I want you to fuck me." I wink at him before padding toward the washroom. Rory trails after me.

"Well, the bathroom is all yours, then. I'd ask top, bottom, or other, but I guess you already answered that."

"Tonight, definitely bottom, but in general, all of the above," I joke as I lean in the washroom doorway and let my eyes wander again. Yeah, I'm excited to get a taste of him. "Want to fuck me once I'm all squeaky clean?"

"Yes, please." Rory licks his lips. His eyes are full of lust as he takes in my nakedness.

"Cool, well, I'm on PrEP, but we should probably use condoms if you've got any," I say.

"I'm not. On PrEP that is, but I got tested last month. I've got condoms and lube in the bedroom. So, I'll be ready when you are." He grins.

"Cool. I'll try not to leave you hanging for too long, then." I lean in to kiss him again. Rory clings to me once more. The heat of his hands on my shoulders tempts me to forgo the shower and just skip to the good part, but I want him to fuck me and that will go better with a bit of prep.

We break apart to catch our breath. Rory looks as pleasure-drunk as I feel, so I grin at him. "Be ready in a minute." With that, I duck into the washroom.

I had a busy schedule today, so I skipped breakfast and lunch, hoping to finish my work in time to hit Adventures early. Downside of that is I'm hungry for more than Rory's dick, but the upshot is that prepping to bottom doesn't take terribly long.

Which is good because I'm horny as fuck and fingering myself in the shower only makes me want him more.

CHAPTER 3

Rory

O h, holy shit, Tate propositioned me. My sexy plumber just asked if I wanted to fuck, kissed me silly, and is currently prepping for sex in my shower. Talk about porn-worthy fantasies coming to life. I fumble around in my suitcase for condoms and lube. I packed them to use with toys for easier cleanup, but now I'm doubly glad that I have them.

If my phallo dick could get hard on its own, I'd be sporting a massive stiffy. Pretty much since he walked through my door. It's been over a year since I got the final stage of my phallo to add the inflatable pump so I can get hard. A couple years since the first operation, and I'm still not entirely used to the giddy knowledge that I can follow through on this flirting without dysphoria about my dick. Or dealing with a messy disclosure conversation. That used to hold me back from casual sex when I still had my natal genitals.

The when, whether to, and how of it all stressed me out too much for casual sex to be worth the effort for me before I got my surgeries. These days, I don't hide that I'm trans, but I also only outright tell people the details when it applies to the conversation. Or if we're close enough for it to matter. It's not like no cis dude has ever had erectile dysfunction, so most guys I've been with have been understanding if I don't come or get hard the way they expect. Not so long as it doesn't interfere with them getting off.

A quickie with my plumber hardly requires getting into my

gender history, even if my heart beat faster when he was looking up at me through his lashes. I can picture him on his knees for very different reasons. The thought of his deep voice calling me daddy does it for me. I adjust my dick and give my balls a little squeeze through my pants to plump up my cock. I might not get hard spontaneously, but the pump that fills up my shaft for sex can mimic a gradual arousal if I time it right. There's a knack to it that I've gotten good at.

Watching Tate fix my bathroom only added to my attraction, oddly enough. There is something compelling about watching someone do something they're skilled at. Tate is unmistakably good at what he does.

I enjoyed listening to him grumbling about the shoddy work that caused the problem with my toilet to happen. It made me feel like I was someone he trusted enough to unburden himself about his workday irritations. Like a friend, or a daddy, even though he was probably just muttering to himself and I just happened to be there. He kept glancing up at me. Almost like a little seeking approval from their caregiver and I found myself offering praise and encouragement every time he checked in with me.

Little or not, Tate pushes those buttons for me. The ones that make me want to take care of my partner. I picture Tate's eyes following my hand, the way he licked his lips like he wished they were on my dick already before he went to shower. Damn, he's hot, with his broad shoulders and imposing bulk.

I want to take him bent over the vanity so I can see his face in the mirror when he comes. Have him on his knees for me while I feed him my cock. I'd love to pound his firm round ass while he begs his daddy to let him come. And I want to kiss him all over when we're done and take care of him.

Whoa, hold on there. I'm getting way ahead of myself. Tate never agreed to my kinks, no matter how much I might want to share them with him. I shake my head, as though that might clear away the fog of lust. It doesn't, but I know better than to spring the daddy thing on someone. This is just a hookup.

It's been a long time since I got to be Kel's caretaker and I miss it. Miss the tenderness of holding her on my lap while she drifts off to sleep after coming her brains out by my hand. I want those sweet, loving moments again with a new partner. But I'm not delusional; the first man to show up at my door will not be my perfect forever boy. I can still sure as shit have some fun with him and give us both a good time tonight.

The sound of running water cuts off and Tate hums to himself as he finishes up in the bathroom. I don't recognize the song, but I'm excited for him to join me. I shuck off my clothing, tossing it onto my open suitcase, before swinging the lid closed. Then I arrange myself on the bed, and roll on the condom. Tate opens the door and steps into the hallway. I give my balls another squeeze to finish inflating my dick, stroking myself as I call out to him. "I'm in here."

Tate pauses in the entryway, leaning against the doorframe in all his naked glory. He's big, muscular in the way of someone who works with his hands for a living. I saw the ease with which he lifted my toilet earlier, so I know he's strong. And that those powerful hands can be gentle.

His gaze on me makes me self-conscious. I hunch my shoulders, unsure whether he'll like what he sees when he looks at me. I might not advertise that I'm trans, but the signs are there, if he knows what to look for. The faded scars from my top surgery and phallo. I'm not ashamed of them, but I am wary of his reaction. Not telling him could be a dangerous misstep, but here we are, too late to turn back now.

"Hey, sexy." Tate strides over to the bed, eager to get back to where we left off before his shower. I let out a relieved breath. Either he doesn't notice or he doesn't care. Both options work for

23

me.

Tate seems totally on board for sex. I reach toward him and he climbs up to straddle my hips. He leans forward for a kiss. I wrap a hand around his nape, holding him in place as I plunder his mouth. My earlier hint of insecurity is gone now, erased by Tate sitting in my lap with our lips joined in a scorching kiss.

I groan at the heat of him on top of me and grind our dicks together. Tate moans into my mouth and bucks his hips forward. I consider taking both our lengths in hand and grinding to completion against him, but I want inside him more than I want a quick orgasm.

I indulge in more kissing, reveling in holding someone in my lap again. I could almost imagine he's my boy, but that's dangerous territory when we haven't discussed it. We will never discuss it; this is a one-night stand. I grip his hips, easing him up to give me room to move. Tate seems to get the idea. He guides my dick between his cheeks and lowers himself onto my lube-slicked shaft.

Our kiss becomes even more heated, my grip on the back of his neck growing more possessive as I sink into Tate, inch by thick, hard inch. The first press of penetration is so much better than my countless fantasies of doing this for real. I'm inside another man. It's not the first time, but that thought is still mind-blowing, looping inside my head and enhancing the perfect pressure of his body clenching around me. The urge to take over and thrust into him with wild abandon is strong, but I keep it in check.

Instead of grabbing him and plunging up into his tight heat, I rest my hands on Tate's thighs and massage his smooth skin. I give him control as he lowers himself all the way down, not stopping until his ass is resting against my hairy thighs. I shift to hold his hips then, needing a moment to let it sink in that I'm really buried balls deep inside of him.

After adjusting to taking my entire length, Tate rocks his hips, easing into fucking himself. He picks up the pace gradually, riding me in slow delicious glides. My pleasure builds with each thrust into his tight heat, but my climax stays just out of reach.

As much as I enjoy the way each languid shift of his body strokes my entire length, it's still hard to resist my urge to take control. The desire to drive the encounter is at odds with the tender part of me that craves taking care of him. Either way, I'm aching to give him what he needs. I want to watch him come apart as he loses himself in the pleasure that I give him. He angles his hips a bit more, moaning at the change in position, and I can't hold back any longer. I buck up, nailing him hard in just the right spot to get him gasping and moaning. Tate's steady movements turn into desperate staccato bounces, seeking more of me.

"Oh, fuck, right there," he moans. So I repeat the motion until he's clinging to my shoulders, his nails digging into my bare skin as he arches and writhes on my dick. His hard cock juts into my belly, painting me in pre-cum. And it's just about the hottest thing I could imagine.

I can't even quantify the number of times I've dreamed about being able to have this. The tight pressure of my partner clenching around my shaft as he rides me. To watch his face on the brink of an orgasm as I thrust my dick in deep. Fuck it, I need better leverage than this position will allow.

I moan and fuck my tongue into his mouth in time with my thrusts. His lips on mine transcend a mere hookup and make this something special. I shift my grip to the back of his neck, holding him in place as I plunder his mouth.

I drink in the way he submits to my kisses. How he opens for me, his tongue meeting mine and chasing after my lips when I pull back. He lets me take all of him, lets me press into his body, utterly intoxicating. I'm not going to fall for a guy just because

I've been inside him. But, oh how good it feels to be able to have this when there were days I never thought I would. His receptive body opening to me is incredible, and he should know it. That I appreciate what he's giving me here.

"You're so tight, so good." I break our kiss to murmur near his ear. "I want to fuck you harder."

"Mhm. Sounds good." Tate agrees, then he catches his lip between his teeth and grinds against me, as if he's reluctant to give up my dick. Wow, that is hot. "I like it hard."

"Lift off me." I rock into him, pressing my shaft more firmly into him as he grinds down and moans. It's still not quite enough. I need to bury myself as deep inside him as I can get. I grip his hips and guide him up off my shaft so that we can roll.

Tate whines at the loss and the plaintive note goes right to my dick and makes me want to give him everything. He makes me feel like I could take on anything with that needy sound. It reminds me of the wonderful sense of taking care of everything my little needs. And how good the sex is when I get to fill that caregiving role with my partner and we're on the same page. This isn't that.

There is nothing kinky about pinning Tate on his back and lifting his legs up to my shoulders as I delve back into his ass. I love taking control, but this is pure vanilla sex. Still, the trust in his eyes as he gazes up at me while he lets me manhandle him into position does things to me. Things that make me wish this wasn't a one-time thing. It's just hot sex with a stranger. Really hot sex. There are definitely worse ways to start a new life in a new city than with the best lay I've had in years.

CHAPTER 4

Tate

Rory pushing me onto my back and bending me in half makes me feel helpless in just the right way. It would be easy to let myself slip into a different headspace, one I don't want right now. I don't want to imagine him lifting my ankles out of the way so he can change my diaper at Adventures. He probably wouldn't want to fuck me if he knew I want that sometimes.

It's not a sexual thing, so I'm not sure why the sex is reminding me of it. It might just be the confident way he rearranges my body. Like he knows what I need and wants to take care of me. I'm probably reading too much into the tenderness in his expression as he positions my body.

I shake my head and try to stay in this moment with him. He holds me tight, lines up and pushes back inside of me. And, oh yes, his firm grip on my hips takes all my control away as he fucks his cock in deep. It's grounding.

This is a hookup, not a scene. He's fucking me, not taking care of me. Then he leans forward enough to kiss me again, bending me uncomfortably and driving in deep. I can't spare anymore mental space to worry about getting attached or what he'd think of my little side as he pounds into me.

"That's it, take it all, baby," Rory murmurs the generic endearment as he snaps his hips forward, then tangles his fingers in my hair for another kiss. I have to remind myself it's generic, not a sign he sees the part of me that's little.

I whimper into his mouth at the overwhelming sense of him taking me that way too. Possessing me and making my body sing with pleasure. This new angle rubs his soft belly against my dick with every thrust. I can feel the rhythmic tightening of his abs under a layer of soft padding. I work a hand between us to get that hint more of the friction I need to come all over him.

He moans as my ass clenches around him and thrusts hard a few more times before he comes too, moaning my name and clinging to me in the aftermath. I let him hold me while I catch my breath, but now that the sex is over, my hips ache from holding this position. I nudge Rory's shoulder and wriggle to free my legs.

He rolls off of me with a groan. "Stick around for another round later?" he offers after flopping onto his back and dealing with the condom.

I glance over at him and his hopeful expression makes me smile. "Sure, I can get it up again in a bit if you feed me first. Didn't grab dinner before coming over here." I scratch my belly and grimace at the sticky mess I made.

"I'll skip the joke about feeding you my dick." Rory sits up and runs his hand through his hair. "Want me to order something? My kitchen is sadly bare."

"Pizza?" I suggest, since it's quick. "Mind if I borrow the washroom again for a minute?"

"Help yourself, running low on towels, though. I've got clean clothes you can borrow if you want to hold off on the coveralls." Rory waves me toward the door. I go to freshen up and Rory follows me. He digs through the cabinet drawers until he finds a washcloth in the third one down and hands it to me. We both wash away the evidence of our sex and get dressed. Rory still looks damn fine in his low-slung sweats. He can't seem to tear his eyes off me in my boxers and a borrowed t-shirt that stretches tight over my shoulders. I suspect he wants me again as much as I want him.

We order a pizza, pick a random show to pretend to watch, and make out on the couch while we wait for dinner to arrive. When it does, we eat with the TV on for background noise. Once the pizza is gone, I run my hand along his thigh. He grins without looking away from the show and moves my hand to his bulge.

He's not hard yet, but as I stroke him and he plays with his balls, his dick stiffens. Rory moves his hand to the front of my pants, slipping past my waistband to grip me in a firm hold. I push into his grip. Neither of us looks away from the TV. It's like we're in some sort of weird staring contest to see who glances away from the screen first. We stroke each other off without breaking the pretense that we're watching TV and it's hot in a way I wouldn't have expected. More about comfort and companionship than being horny. Neither of us looks away from the screen as we stroke each other to orgasm.

Afterward, Rory gives me one last kiss. I'm not sure if I should leave, but he pulls me into his arms and I can't resist the excuse for a snuggle. He lets me nestle back against his chest as we finish the episode of the show that neither of us was actually watching. When the credits roll, he's snoring softly with his chin resting on my head.

I extricate myself from his comforting hold. It's hard to leave his embrace. I've wished I could fall asleep on a daddy of my own just like this countless times. But Rory isn't my daddy. He isn't even a big. He's just a guy who likes to snuggle after he comes. There go my stupid emotions, getting all attached over nothing.

I pad away to wash up again, then change out of my borrowed shirt and back into my less than pristine coveralls. No sense waking Rory up before I leave. It will be easier to make a clean break of it. Even if the sex was the best I've had in a while.

One night of amazing sex isn't worth getting involved with him. Not worth the risk of getting attached when I doubt someone outside the scene will understand my need to be little sometimes. I drag my feet about getting ready, considering leaving him my card so he can get in touch if he wants a repeat. But I know me and that's not a good idea. I gather my gear from the doorway, hesitating over sneaking off for longer than is sensible. I leave him sleeping on the couch with the TV streaming another episode in the background.

CHAPTER 5

Rory

A full week into my new life and I'm convinced this was the right move for me. My job is everything I'd hoped and more. I've got contracts lined up for months of steady work and a great recording studio space to use. Vancouver is the place to be for the industry these days.

I haven't made much progress on finding long-term housing yet, but part of that is a stupidly persistent desire not to sever that last tenuous connection with Tate. My hookup with the sexy plumber left a mark. There was just something about him I can't get out of my head. I mentioned him to Kel when we spoke. Her response was to encourage me to get connected with the local kink scene, if I'm so eager to take care of someone. And I can admit to myself that was part of the appeal.

It isn't just great sex that has me revisiting that night in my fantasies all week long. It's the vulnerable way Tate gazed up at me as I positioned him where I wanted and drove into him. How he let me hold him after we came the second time, the warm weight of his body utterly pliant in my arms while he snuggled into my chest. The familiar routine from when Kel and I dated, making a special treat of sitting to watch a cartoon together and pizza in the living room. His rapt attention on the TV every time I snuck a glance at him reminded me of being with a little. The cartoon we picked wasn't necessarily for kids, but it still made me want that again.

So, after my chat with Kel and my inability to get my night

with Tate out of my head, I take the plunge. Sort of. I at least message the organizer for a local munch to see if it's alright for me to swing by the event to meet people. Turns out there are several options available locally.

The most promising one is geared toward bigs, littles, and pups. The organizers are a pup and their Mommy. QutiePup messages me back with an enthusiastic invite to join them. They send me a barrage of messages about the event. Each one had a liberal sprinkling of excited punctuation about welcoming a new member to the community. They have me charmed and eager to meet them in person after our chat online.

The day of the munch, I almost chicken out at least half a dozen times. Work is amazing, but getting used to a new place is always an adjustment and I'm tired by the time Friday rolls around. Excuses flit through my mind as I decide which way to turn at the corner. Left to the bus home or across the street, toward the restaurant and my potential new friends.

What eventually has me turning away from my usual bus back to my generic temporary apartment is QutiePup. They seemed so excited; I don't want to disappoint them by no-showing. Then again, I could PM them to let them know not to expect me. I'm overthinking this. I have to eat dinner, regardless.

The worst-case scenario is that I decide the group isn't for me and I order my food to go. No one is going to bite me. Probably. At least not without my consent.

I cross the street to the stop that will take me to the munch. For a while, navigating to the restaurant occupies my mind. I don't want to miss my stop and I'm not familiar with the area. Once I find the generic chain restaurant, I have to nerve myself up to walk through the front door. I tell the staff member who greets me I'm here to meet a group. They don't give any visible reaction, sweeping an arm toward the reserved event space in the back of the dining area. I thank them and go to see if I can make some new friends.

I recognize QutiePup right away from their profile pictures. They're standing with a couple of other people. A pudgy redhead with long hair and a cute dinosaur t-shirt waves in my direction.

"Hey, new person!" The redhead greets me loudly.

"Oh, are you DaddyRoar? Hi! I'm so glad you could make it," QutiePup bounces over to greet me as if I'm their long lost best friend. I smile at their puppyish enthusiasm as they offer me a hand to shake.

"Hi. That's me. I'm Rory when I'm offline." I smile. We already exchanged pronouns online, so I don't bother with that again.

"Oh, cool. I'm Quent. Most folks here call me Q, though. Want to meet everyone?" Q gestures toward the other people. Most of them are chatting over an array of appetizers. "Mommy let me order cheese fries, if you want to share some? Or there are wings coming, too."

"Do you usually all share?" I ask, trailing after Q and unsure of the etiquette with a new group of people. When I went to meet Kel and Tamara's friends at their local munch, we all ordered our own food.

"The appetizers, yeah, sometimes. With this group, anyway. It's a small gathering most months, so we are all up in each other's business. Anyway, this is Monty and Connor, they're both littles and they both use he/him pronouns. Guys, this is Rory. He's new to the city."

Both boys eye me up and down. Monty's gaze lingers on my bulge. Connor is more demure about checking me out, but he looks, too. "Hello there, Daddy," Monty purrs. He's cute, if a little forward.

Q gives their friend's shoulder a shove. "He never said you could call him that, Monty. Play nice."

Monty pouts. "I'm always nice."

"Only when you aren't busy being naughty," Q counters. "Let Rory sit and have some of my tasty treats."

"You just want him to *be* your tasty treat at our next play date." Monty grumbles. "Don't let the innocent face fool you, Rory. Q's a total slut."

"Takes one to know one," Q shoots back as they reclaim their seat between Connor and Monty. They're both grinning at the banter, so I take it neither of them thinks that's a bad thing. Q stuffs their mouth full of cheese fries and moans obscenely over the food. "So good."

A woman I recognize from Q's profile as their mommy excuses herself from a knot of other people who she was talking to and heads toward us with pursed lips.

"And you say I have bad manners?" Monty rolls his eyes as he uses his foot to shove the chair next to him out for me. "Join us?"

"Um, sure." I accept the offered seat, not sure how to take their banter or if I should take Q up on the offer to share the fries.

"Are you a daddy?" Connor asks, without quite looking at me.

"I'd like to be." I answer honestly. Connor nods.

"Cool. It's always fun to have new people to play with. Oh, hi, Miss Kylee." Connor waves and Q freezes with their mouth still full of fries.

"Are you behaving, pup?" Kylee asks as she hooks a finger through Q's collar. The dark leather presses into the pup's neck and they squirm.

"Yes, Mommy."

"Hm, because it looks like you forgot your table manners. We've discussed this."

"Sorry, Mommy."

"Mhm, somehow I doubt that. We'll have to work on your eating out skills when we get home, won't we?" There is a gleam in her eye that makes the words seem more like a promise than a threat as she releases Q's collar and ruffles their hair.

"Yes, Mommy." Q licks their lips, then turns their head to kiss their Mommy's hand before she withdraws her touch.

"Are you my good pup?" She twists her wrist around to pat Q's cheek.

Q nods.

"Then introduce me to our new friend." Kylee tips her head toward me.

"This is Rory. He's a big who wants to play with us, don't you, Rory?" Q grins at me, mischief dancing in their eyes.

"I'd like that. For now, I'm just dipping my toes back into kink after a bit of a hiatus." I glance between Q and the others.

"Oh, was there a reason for that?" Kylee rests one proprietary hand on her pup's head and the other on Connor's shoulder. A nonverbal warning that she is there to protect them from any skeletons I might have lurking in my closet. At a glance, Connor's compact muscular frame makes him look like he doesn't need the tall, willowy Kylee to protect him from anything. But the boy glances up at her appreciatively. Like he's used to not being seen for himself. That's something to remember if we play together. Not to take the sleek, gym-honed muscles peeking out from his sleeveless shirt to mean he wants to be treated like a tough guy.

"I took a break to work through some personal issues. Nothing to do with kink or anything that happened in a scene. I'm thinking of applying for membership at Adventures, but I wanted to meet some of the bigs and littles who play there first, that's all. Like I told Quent."

Kylee nods. "Great. Martin sometimes joins us at these events. I'll introduce you if he shows up later."

"He's the club owner?" I ask. The name sounds familiar.

"That's right. Great guy, very safety focused." Kylee squeezes Connor's shoulder and pats Q's head again, which the pup leans into as if they want nothing more than to be stroked and fussed over.

"Sounds good." I smile at the affection between the two of them.

"Good, can we eat my treat now, Mommy?" Q interjects with a longing look at the food.

"You hungry, pup?" Kylee musses Q's hair and they nod.

"Show me your good manners, then." Kylee takes the open seat beside her pup. Q reaches for the stack of small plates and hands them around to Kylee, Connor, Monty, and me.

"Dig in." They gesture to the platter of cheesy fries and I unwrap a fork from a rolled up napkin to take a few along with the others. Q waits until everyone else has filled their plates before glancing to their mommy for permission to load their own plate.

Kylee nods and Q takes several forkfuls, then several more, until Kylee pats the pup's hand. "That's enough."

"Okay, Mommy. Thanks for the treats." Q leans in to kiss her cheek, then tucks into their food.

The fries are tasty. Not quite amazing enough to warrant Q's pornographic moans over them, but I guess if they're a special treat that could make anything taste better. Kylee is watching her pup like she'd love nothing more than to devour them with the same enthusiasm Q has for the fries.

"So, Rory, was it? Are you enjoying Vancouver so far?" Kylee asks, turning to face me.

"Yes, I'm loving it here. The views are amazing, the traffic isn't half as bad as I expected with the bridges and all, and the vibe here is very chill. Plus, it's nice to meet you all. It's been a long time since I've had a little to take care of and I've missed that."

"Well, there are lots of us at the club." Monty grins at me. "The four of us are besties, but we aren't the only littles who play at Adventures."

"That's great to hear." I smile at him.

"Would you want to play with me sometime?" Monty bats his eyes at me.

I chuckle at his guilelessness. "I'd like that, Monty."

"Speaking of the four of us, is Tate coming tonight?" Connor stacks his and Monty's empty plates, then reaches to add Kylee's to the pile when she nods that she's done, too.

My ears perk up at the name. It's not exactly common, but I doubt the guy I hooked up with after he fixed my toilet is the same person Connor is talking about. There's no way.

Monty wipes his mouth on a napkin before answering. "He said he had to finish up at the bathroom renovation that's been having all the issues. The clients don't like the way the clear epoxy he used around the toilet install clashes with the grout color or something ridiculous like that. I swear he gets the weirdest clients." He gestures with his fork as he talks.

Oh, hell. So this Tate also works with plumbing. There could be thousands of plumbers named Tate, though. No guarantee it's the same guy.

"Oh, hey, there he is!" Monty stands to wave his friend over to us. I turn to follow his gaze right to the same sexy plumber I was balls deep inside of a few days ago. What are the odds a sweet boy with connections to the local kink community would all but fall onto my dick on my first night in my new city? This has to be a sign from the universe. A neon flashing green light that I'm on the right path with my life.

Tate catches sight of me and falters, but then he gives me a tentative smile and strides over to the table. He nods to Kylee, hugs Monty, ruffles Q's hair, and gives Connor a quick clap on the back as they all exchange happy greetings. Then he turns to face me, and I can't read his expression well enough to say if he's glad to see me. "Didn't expect to see you here."

"What are the odds?" I grin at him. What a serendipitous turn of events that the guy I can't stop fantasizing about since we fucked the night away shares my kinks. I just hope my showing up unexpectedly isn't an issue for him.

"Oooh. Do you two know each other?" Monty leans on Tate's shoulder as he looks between us. I hold my tongue to see how Tate wants to handle this situation. "I'm sensing a story. Spill Tater-Tot."

"Nothing much to tell, Monty. I met him on a service call," Tate shrugs. "Toilet working for you?"

"Yep, thanks again." I quash the irrational thought that I could say I need him to take another look at my plumbing. He's worth asking out properly. I want to make my intentions clear, now that fate's giving me a second chance to connect with him. Especially if we can bring the chemistry from our hookup to a scene.

I can just imagine what it might be like to hold him close and tickle him until he squirms. Or settle him on my lap for a story while he snuggles in a cute pajama. I want to watch his adult worries and stress fall away as he settles into my home to color. I want to play games with him, read him stories, cuddle for cartoons, and whatever else he likes to do when he's little. If he's little. Monty implied as much, but I'd rather hear it from Tate. I hope he wants me the way I want him.

"So, I take it you realize that this is a munch for people who are into age play and puppy play, right?" Tate asks, his entire focus on me.

"Yeah, I'm aware." I nod. "I'm a daddy."

Tate cracks a smile. "Yay. I mean. We could still play if we were both little, but..."

"But you'd rather have a daddy to take care of you than another playmate?" I suggest, hoping that means he's as into the idea of spending more time together as I am.

"Yeah." Tate nods.

"Oh, Tatey-Tot made a new friend." Monty nudges Tate toward me. Tate swats his friend's hand away, but he takes the seat next to me.

"Hey, look! Martin brought something." Q points as a tall Black man enters the room with a messenger bag slung over his shoulder.

"Score! Wanna bet it's more coloring books like last time?" Monty is already walking toward the new arrival as he talks, all thought of teasing Tate and me gone at the new distraction. Q and Connor go with him to see what sort of fun Martin has brought.

Tate chuckles low. "So, that's Monty, going full throttle at whatever new shiny thing catches his eye. Are you settling into the city alright?" Tate asks as he grabs a few of the remaining cheese fries.

"Yep, loving it here." I nod. Tate smiles at me and we talk about all the things I just have to do now that I'm here. He points out unique quirks of living in Vancouver and the parts of the city he loves best.

This is the same small talk I've done with practically everyone

I've met this week, but it feels different with Tate. As if he might actually care about my opinion of his city. Or maybe it's that I want him to care. It's not just the city that's making me feel like I've found a home, either. Here in this chain restaurant with a group of strangers that I'm hoping could become my friends, I'm thinking I might have the space to be my authentic self. A self with nothing to hide and no shame, and that's freeing in a way I've only caught glimpses of before.

CHAPTER 6

Tate

The last person I expected to see at the monthly big, little, and pup munch that Q and Kylee organize is sitting with my friends. I never thought I'd see Rory again after our night together. Not that he didn't rock my world. I just figured we had little in common beyond a few shared orgasms. Guess I was dead wrong about that.

For a gut-roiling second, I wonder if he somehow knew I'd be here and tracked me down. That's something Gary would have done. When we first met, he kept showing up wherever I went, sometimes even at job sites. When I confronted him, he insisted that installing a tracking app on my phone without permission was a romantic gesture. And naïve as I was, I believed him. I didn't recognize the red flags with his unnegotiated controlling behavior until after the relationship ended.

The look of surprise on Rory's face when our eyes meet—followed by the warm smile that stretches his lips—tells the entire story. He's as surprised as I am. And it's a pleasant surprise. That puts some pep in my step as I go to join him where he's sitting with my closest friends. Rory hasn't done a thing to deserve comparing him to Gary. And he's happy to see me here.

Monty ribs me about knowing the new big in town, which is fine because Rory can't seem to take his eyes off me. We make the usual small talk while my friends run off to take their pick of the new coloring books Martin brought along for the night.

Normally, I'd be squirming to go join them so I could lose

41

myself in coloring for a while. It's not quite the same as regressing at the club, but it would still be a nice mental break from the grind of adulting. Except I'd rather sit here with Rory and chat about mundane crap than color. Then he tells me about his job and I can't help a delighted little sound as I grab his arm.

"Oh, wow, you mean you're really the voice of a video game character?"

"Several." He nods. "And some cartoon characters. I've also worked on commercials."

"Okay, so tell me someone you've voiced," I ask, not expecting much.

"Hmm." Rory rubs his chin as he considers. "I think the most popular character I've done to date is Dale from *Dinoblox*. And some people recognize me as Sparkles from *Pup Adventures*, once I tell them." His voice shifts to a higher, more nasally register and he speaks faster as he says the last sentence. I recognize the overeager pup's voice from the show that Q is obsessed with.

"Really?" I clap in delight. "Oh my god, Q is going to flip. They love that show." I wave to my friend, trying to catch Quent's eye. "Hey, Q, come here," I call, raising my voice when they don't notice me waving.

My outburst earns me a warning look from Ms. Kylee, who is standing beside Q. She isn't my mommy, but we have an agreement where she looks out for me and the rest of Q's friends when we don't have a caretaker. And I'm being too loud for the restaurant. I give her a sheepish look and mouth an apology.

"Sorry," I say to Rory, with my inside voice. I glance at Kylee and she gives me a smile and a nod at my quieter voice. Quent heads toward us with interested curiosity at my excitement. "Quent loves Sparkles. They'll want your autograph when you tell them. Bet you get that a lot?"

"Not really." Rory chuckles. "I'm not an actual celebrity."

"You're good, though." I nod at him. "And you sound way different as a pup."

"What's up? Who sounds different as a pup?" Q asks, as they come up behind my chair and lean on my shoulders to peer over my head at Rory.

"Rory." I gesture at him, then realize that my meaning isn't clear, given who I'm talking to. "I mean, he's not a pup like you. Tell him, Rory. About Sparkles."

"Tate means my Sparkles voice isn't the same as my speaking voice. I try to mix things up with my characters." Rory rescues me from having to explain. "I'm a voice actor."

"And you play Sparkles?" Q bounces, jostling my shoulders.

"Technically, I voice him. A cocker spaniel named Gravy plays Sparkles on the show." Rory laughs.

"He's so pretty. I like his curly ears. Can you do his voice?" Quent bats their eyes at Rory.

"Sure. Hello, Q, what's your favorite puppy treat?" Rory asks in his character voice.

Q grins and flashes me his most mischievous smile. "Bones, duh."

I shove my friend. "Gross. They mean boners. Q is all about giving head."

"I'm good at it too," Q boasts.

Rory clears his throat and I'm not sure if he's amused or embarrassed by this turn in conversation. "Does your Mommy let you have those kinds of treats often?"

"Yeah. She likes to watch me play." Quent shrugs. "She lets me have most of the things I like. Except a bio dog. I like your Sparkles voice. Mommy says we can't get a dog like Sparkles because they might chew up my toys and shed everywhere."

"And your mommy knows that you're allergic to dog fur," I point out helpfully.

"I could take allergy meds." Quent flops into the seat beside me and pouts. They lean forward to dig through the last few bits of cheese and toppings left on the platter in front of me for any hidden fries.

"You could, but they make you sleepy." I remind them.

"So? I'd get used to it. Can't be as bad as having a defective thyroid. Score!" Quent holds up a soggy fry in triumph before gobbling their find. "You should come to Adventures for our next littles' night, Rory. Tate would love to have a daddy to take care of him."

"I'd like that, too." Rory agrees. As if it's that simple. Maybe it is.

"We could still play together, even if it's not specifically a littles' night. I go most weekends." I flash him a hopeful smile.

"But you rarely play on the weekends." Q interjects, wiggling in their seat. "You should get them to play, Rory." Q adds with a cheeky grin. I nudge them under the table, trying to convince them to butt out of it. Sometimes Q is just as bad as Monty about pushing too hard and saying impulsive things they shouldn't.

"I'd love to arrange a play date with you at the club," Rory agrees. "Let me take your number so we can arrange the details." He pulls up his contacts and I recite my number for him.

"Yeah, okay." I flash him a smile. "Text me, so I have yours, too." He does, and we hold each other's gazes for a long moment, until Hope, one of the other bigs, comes over to introduce herself. Her little, Angel, is here too. But they are with most of the other littles where they've gathered around Martin and his coloring books.

"Come on, Tate. Martin found a book with Pup Adventures characters this week, and Trish is eyeing it, so if we want it, we better claim it." Q tugs me toward the books and I let them lead me away from Rory. "Always leave them wanting more." Quent leans in to whisper at me once we're out of earshot of my crush.

They might be right, but I can't help a glance back over my shoulder at Rory. He's watching me, smiling and talking animatedly with Hope and another mommy I don't know well. Q jostles me until I turn around to join them with the coloring books.

For a while, I lose myself in scribbling with the other littles. Q claims two pictures of Sparkles for us and the familiar routine of sitting with my crayons while the bigs chat helps my adult worries fall into the background. Monty teases me about how meticulous I'm being. "You take forever, Tate. Look, I've finished three of the dinosaurs and you're still working on your first picture."

"Because you scribble and I want to make mine perfect." I stick out my tongue at him.

"But I want the gold you're using for my *Monoclonius* horn and you are taking for*ever!*" he whines.

I glance over at him and I'm pretty sure it is taking all his willpower not to just snatch the crayon out of my hand. His fingers twitch and he fiddles with the edge of his drawing. "Here, you can borrow it." I pass my crayon to him with a heavy sigh and look for a different shade of brown to finish coloring Sparkles. He's an in-between shade of brownish gold, anyway. Rory will probably still like my picture.

"Score! You're the best, Tater-Tot. Thanks." Monty happily scrawls gold all over his dinosaur's face. I shake my head and find the right shade of tan to continue my picture.

"That was kind of you," Martin praises me. I flash him a smile.

It's nice to be surrounded by people who understand me. I enjoy coloring with the others, even if they all finish their pictures before me and move on to other things.

"You're doing a great job staying in the lines," Kylee observes when Quent scampers away to show Trish and Angel some new toy they brought along tonight. "Sparkles looks just like on the show." She rubs a circle on my back and I lean into the touch. I'm not nearly as tactile as Q, but sometimes it's nice to be touched like this. Just pure affection.

"I'm kind too!" Monty pipes up. "I'm helping him not be so uptight about his picture." He discards the gold crayon, the tip significantly blunted from the amount of pressure he used, in favor of a green one for his background. Despite his crimes against crayons, I can't help smiling at my bestie. He always has my back, even if his logic makes no sense.

"Sure, Monty. You're certainly something, anyway." Kylee tugs on Monty's ponytail to take the sting out of the teasing, and he grins at her.

I want to fall into the headspace where I can bask in Kylee's admiration of my picture, but it just isn't happening. Martin and Kylee's affirmations feel hollow tonight. It takes until I'm finished with my picture, every detail colored to perfection, to realize why their kind words don't fill me with pride as much as usual. It's not coming from the person I want.

I want *my* daddy to praise my pictures. For once, I can't make that crucial detail stop mattering. The futility of the realization leaves me grumpy and restless. I give up on coloring another picture and debate whether to sign my name in the grass under Sparkles's paws.

I don't normally bother with signing my pictures like some of the other littles. Part of me wants my name on this one, even if the letters are a jumbled mess and I get the 'E' backwards like usual. My crappy handwriting doesn't matter as much when I'm little, but I still cringe every time I have to reveal my issues with letters. Still, part of me wants to tell Rory, so there isn't anything scary left hanging over us. Not that I'm giving him the picture or anything. That would be weird, right?

I glance between the picture and Rory, wondering if he'd like it, before tucking it into my bag for later. I've fantasized about a daddy who wants to display my artwork and tell me how good I am often. It's jarring to have a specific person in mind when I imagine what he'd say about the way I colored Sparkles' fur. Would Rory notice how I added the pattern from his collar on the show to the plain band in the printout? Funny to picture it pinned to his fridge in that cookie cutter condo where we had awesome sex instead of my familiar old one.

I'm not sure how to feel about how attracted I am to Rory, other than that I'm fixing to fall hard and fast if I let myself. The rest of the night, I catch Rory stealing glances my way. Even as he gets introduced around the gathering, his eyes keep finding me. It's not every week we get new people joining our little group, so I get why everyone wants to meet him. There aren't a ton of us, but enough that it's got to be overwhelming to be the new person. I don't want to add to that.

I have his number now, so we can chat again later. When he isn't getting swept up in the excitement of meeting others who share our kinks.

CHAPTER 7

Tate

When it comes to Rory, I apparently have zero chill. I wait until I get home from the munch to text him a silly good night GIF with a teddy bear. Restraint? What restraint?

Then I overthink the message. Will Rory think I'm being too forward? I've played with bigs who prefer to be the one to start anything. But most of them weren't a good fit for me. I don't want to come across as desperate. I just really like him. And the cute bear reminded me of being tucked into bed with a stuffie on the rare occasions I have a big to play with me like that.

Sometimes, when Q and Kylee host play parties, I've stayed over at their place. Kylee will tuck me into their guest bed if it gets too late, or the weather is bad. Often those nights end with Monty and Connor snuggled in next to me. But a cuddle pile isn't what I want with Rory. And the teddy bear is as much as saying I want him to tuck me into bed. Or is it?

Despite how much I hate texting, I'm sorely tempted to send him a lengthy explanation that the teddy bear doesn't mean anything. Then I bite my lip and stare at my phone like a kid with a crush, half wishing I could unsend the message before he sees it. The other half is hoping he'll reply right away so I can stop worrying about how he'll react to my message.

It's way too soon to get so invested in him, but I like how he made me feel valued and cared for when we screwed around.

Rory feeding me pizza and holding me tight after we jerked each other off is fantasy fodder. He treated me the way I imagine my daddy taking care of me. I liked his rapt attention on me while he watched me work in his washroom. The way he focused on me like I was the only one who mattered when we were chatting earlier. How he kept stealing glances at me all night long, but also seemed to get along with my friends.

Q tried to cajole me into giving Rory my Sparkles picture, hinting that it was a fridge-worthy offering and jostling me until Rory had left. I gave Monty a ride home. He spent most of the drive teasing me about having a crush. Until I turned the tables and ever so innocently mentioned that Luke had been tight-lipped about what he did at littles' night last week other than to say he enjoyed his evening.

I'm not clueless. I know Monty has a thing for my brother. Even if Quent hadn't told me about the two of them playing in a private room, I can guess at what's between the lines. When the usually chatty Monty doesn't have much to say about his latest conquest, it means something. Luke would be good for him. It's harder to say if Monty would be good for Luke. Okay, lies, I know Monty would be naughty for Luke. But I could see that working for the two of them.

My brother can be firm when he needs to, but he's also one of the kindest and most patient people I know. He'd be a great daddy for my best friend and I think Monty could be just the sort of boy Luke really needs. One who can challenge him just enough to keep them both satisfied without pushing Luke too far.

I just don't like to think of Luke in that context. That's something I need to get used to, if he and Monty keep hanging out, I guess. I don't want to lose out on my playtime with Monty. If he and Luke are going to be a thing, then I'll just have to learn to live with watching my brother getting kinky. It's not like he's got anything I haven't seen before. And if I play my cards right,

Monty might not be the only one to find a daddy of his own.

My phone startles me out of my idle fantasies of Monty and me both finding our perfect daddies at the same time. Rory isn't my daddy. Not yet. But he could be. I jab at the text-to-speech toggle and get it to read his message to me.

Rory: Hi, Tate. Cute bear. Is there a special stuffie that you're snuggled up with tonight?

There is a bit of a pause, long enough to give me a chance to reply, before he follows up with a second text. Followed by a goodnight GIF of his own with a cartoon cow jumping over the moon.

Rory: Sorry if that's too personal to ask? Good night to you, too.

I bite my lip and consider how to reply. The dictation on my phone does a crap job with longer messages. I hate having to speak the punctuation, too. And I'm not ready to tell him I struggle with reading, so I snap a picture of Fuzzy sitting on my pillows. I hit send before I can overthink just how intimate it is to share the threadbare stuffed penguin nestled into my bed.

My mom bought Fuzzy for me when I was a baby. Something to do with me being the best hockey souvenir ever. Which, gross. But also weirdly sweet. Mom has a way of oversharing.

Fuzzy has been with me my entire life, and it shows. He's loved bald where I rub his smooth beak to help me get to sleep when I'm stressed. One of his eyes is now a shiny black button, and his left wing had to be sewn back on after a mishap with my uncle's dog when I was nine. There's a patch from where Mom cut him open in an ill-conceived effort to add extra stuffing after hundreds of trips through the wash. And I just sent a picture of him to a potential date. I hide my face in my hands, holding my breath for his reaction.

Rory doesn't leave me hanging for long. My phone reads his

message.

Rory: Aw, what's this little cutie's name?

Tate: Fuzzy.

I type it out, even though the tiny letters dance in front of my eyes frustratingly because I don't trust the software to get the name right. I should just call Rory. It would be easier to get to know him with a voice chat.

Rory: Love it. Fuzzy the...um, penguin?

Tate: Yes. Call me?

I hug my phone to my chest while I wait anxiously for his response. So many guys our age prefer to text. I've had a few give me a hard time about my strong preference for calling. Most of my friends are the same way, but they make an exception for me since it's easier for me to process a phone call. Especially if they have a lot to say or need a quick response.

My phone buzzes against my chest.

"Hello?" I answer on the first ring. Overeager much? But I *am* eager to talk to him, and maybe it's not a bad thing to let him know that.

"Hi. It's Rory." Rory's voice in my ear while I'm lying in bed in my PJs feels intimate.

"I figured." I roll onto my back and hug Fuzzy under my chin.

"Right." He chuckles self-consciously. "So, what's up? Or did you just want to hear my voice again?"

"You got me. I mean, are you surprised? Isn't your voice why they pay you the big bucks?" I tease him.

"I don't know about big bucks, but it pays the bills." Rory laughs, which makes me grin, too.

"But for serious, I had fun talking with you earlier."

"I did too. So, tell me more about Fuzzy?" Rory asks.

"You really want to hear about my stuffie?" I check.

"Yep. Looks like he's very well loved. So tell me about him." Rory sounds sincere, so I take him at his word that he's really interested.

I consider where to start. "Well, he's an Adélie penguin. I got him as a baby. He was the inspiration for several of my grade school research papers. And the reason I was obsessed with *Scamper the Penguin* as a kid."

"That's the one with the pink and blue baby penguins adrift on an iceberg, right? And they had to make their way home?" Rory checks.

"Yep." I nod, even though he can't see me. "I swear I wore out the VHS tape re-watching that movie as a kid."

"Yeah? I'd have thought VHS tapes were a little before your time." Rory asks.

"Before my time? Pretty sure we're close to the same age. How old do you think I am?"

"I'd say you're mid-twenties?" Rory guesses.

"Be specific. I'd pin you at just under thirty?"

Rory sighs. "The tribulations of having a boyish face; I'm thirty-three. It's not so bad here, since the drinking age is nineteen, but in the US I pretty much always get carded if I try to buy alcohol. It's a pain." Rory says that like it's some huge hardship instead of a minor inconvenience, but I guess having a baby face might get old after a while. Or if the trans pride pronoun pin I saw him wearing and his scars mean that his ID didn't always match his appearance, showing it to people probably sucked. Not that I'm going to bring that up. His gender history is his story to tell, or keep to himself. "And I'd guess you're twenty-four, if I have to pick a specific number."

"Close, twenty-five." I correct him. "So, you're eight years older than me, not too much of a gap, right?"

"Right." Rory agrees.

"As to the VHS thing, Mom had to be pretty thrifty when I was little. My dad wasn't in the picture and he wasn't always the best about paying his child support at first." That's the diplomatic way of saying it took threats of the tabloids and courts getting involved for him to contribute to my upbringing. "She and my uncle stockpiled a bunch of old tapes when the video rental place near us had a big sale because they switched to DVDs. So that's pretty much what I grew up with."

"Hm. Do you still have a copy?"

"I might? It's been ages since I last watched it. Mom is a bit of a packrat, though. The tape might be in her basement if my step-mom didn't convince her to let it go during their last cleaning spree. Not sure we have anything that can still play it."

"That's a shame. But wait, you have two moms?"

"Yep. Funny story actually, my brother Luke is actually my step-brother and we hooked up before our moms introduced us to each other."

"No shit?" Rory chuckles. "Small world. Bet it's nice having queer family."

"For sure." I agree. "Never had to worry about coming out, since I always knew Mom is bi and she made a point of never assuming I'd be into girls or guys or anyone, really."

"That's great. My family never seemed to know what to do with me. I'm the only out one that I know of. It doesn't always feel like they get me, or why I moved so far away from the conservative rural area where I grew up. But anyway. If we can find *Scamper*, I'd like to watch it with you."

"Yeah? You'd want to have a movie night with me? Like, as a little?"

"If you'd want to share that part of yourself with me, I'd like that very much, Tate."

"I'd like to. If we can't find Scamper, they've made plenty of other penguin movies. I like the Madagascar ones. The movies and the TV show spin off." It would be easy to slip into that headspace and gush about my favorite penguin movies. Too easy. Rory has a certain tranquility that puts me at ease.

"I'm pretty sure they make that show here in Vancouver," he muses. "The industry is growing here."

"Guess that's why you moved here?" I stifle a yawn.

"It is."

"And you think you'll be around a while?" Please let him agree. At the munch, he mentioned moving up and down the West Coast for work before settling in LA when we chatted earlier. I don't want him to leave before we can see where this might lead.

"Definitely."

"Okay. Good." I yawn again. This time I can't hold it back. It's been a long week and as much as I wish I could stay up talking to Rory all night, it's getting late.

"I think so, too. You sound sleepy. Why don't you get some rest and I can call you again tomorrow?"

"Tell me a bedtime story first?" I yawn again.

Rory chuckles. "I don't have any stories on me at the moment, little one."

There's trepidation in his tone. And that makes me realize that I'm asking him to put me to bed. Like a Daddy would. Which might cross some lines since we haven't explicitly agreed to play like that. Not tonight, anyway.

"Sorry. No pressure."

"No, don't be sorry. I'm just not sure what you want from me, Tate."

"I'd like to see if you'd want to be my daddy. But I don't want to assume anything and I know we haven't discussed anything like that. So, yeah."

"And if I was your daddy, you'd want me to read you a bedtime story?"

"Yeah."

"I'll have to see about getting some penguin books for you, then."

"Really?" I squeeze Fuzzy to contain my excitement.

"Really. If you want me to call you and read you a bedtime story, I can do that."

"Nice, my own personal full service daddy. Puts a new spin on the term service call." I laugh at my joke, though it makes me flash to vivid memories of my call out to his place and our spectacular first night together. I am definitely not opposed to a repeat of that night, via telephone or in person.

Rory clears his throat. The roughness in his voice makes me think I might not be the only one thinking of our night together. "Yeah, about that. Since you brought it up, I'm interested in you, Tate. More than just getting off together."

"As a potential little? Or boyfriend? Or just a scene partner?" I press my lips to Fuzzy's head to keep from getting too worked up about his reply.

"All the above? I want to date you and get to know you. And part of that is getting to know your little side, too. I'm looking for a partner who shares my kinks and my life."

"I want that," another huge yawn interrupts my sentence, "too. A daddy who takes care of me when I'm little and a lover who still sees me as his equal."

"Good. Then I guess we're on the same page for now. We can discuss it in more depth when you aren't falling asleep."

"Cool. Talk more tomorrow?"

"Yes," Rory agrees. "Now, are you ready for bed?"

"Mhm." I stifle a yawn.

"Then it's time for my good boy to go to sleep."

"M'kay. Good night, Daddy," I mumble, freezing when I realize what slipped out of my mouth. But he said he wants to be my daddy, and the title feels right when I murmur it to him.

"Good night, little one." Rory replies. It could just be that I'm overtired, but he sounds softer, more tender, when he says the endearment. Like I'm something precious to be treasured. I hang up, turn on an episode of Pup Adventures to stave off the emptiness of my lonely apartment, and drift off to sleep with Rory's voice in my ears.

CHAPTER 8

Rory

T he next couple of weeks fly past in a blur of getting used to my new job, finding permanent housing, and getting to know some new friends online. The munch was the perfect way to meet people, and I have a few invites to get together for coffee or drinks. I have Martin's number to arrange a tour of Adventures whenever I'm free, but I have to prioritize my housing search. Which is turning out more difficult than I expected.

After two weeks of fruitless searching and countless listings that either didn't work for me or ended up getting rented before I could put in an application, I finally found a sublet. A friend of a coworker needed to move as soon as possible, so I lucked into the perfect apartment at a reasonable price. The new place isn't huge, but it's mostly furnished. That's a huge bonus since I hardly brought anything with me from the US. So my move only takes one trip by car and a bit of a shopping spree to grab the essentials I don't have yet. Like towels and a coffee maker.

Now that I've had some time to explore, I'm loving the location in Kitsilano. It is convenient to work, beaches, restaurants, and anything else I could want. Not to mention, it isn't too far from Adventures.

With my move complete, I can finally focus on more interesting pursuits. Namely, Tate. I didn't have time to talk to him alone again at the munch after Q hustled my sexy plumber off to color. But we've been texting daily ever since that night.

He's even started calling me before bed.

It's still early days, but I'm into him. And I fell for him a little more the first time he ended our call with a shy, 'goodnight, daddy.' Those words made me want to be his daddy for real, not just on the phone. It's a shame we've both been too busy to meet up in person again. I want our first official date to be special.

Tate mostly sends me funny GIFs and replies to my longer messages with one or two-word answers. I get the impression he isn't a huge fan of texting, so most of the time we save any serious conversation for his nightly calls. Anytime he sends me more than a handful of words, the messages are littered with typos or wrong words. He seems to apologize for it every time, too. I've assured him I don't mind the typos. I saw that he uses the speech-to-text feature when he's working, so it's not even his fault that it messes up or leaves out punctuation. Plus, I couldn't care less about his spelling; I just like hearing from him. Whenever his name pops up on my phone, it makes me smile.

Even when the buzz of my notifications goes off after we say goodnight. Like last night, when he sent me a silly GIF of a busted pipe geysering water. He followed that up with a cute dog jumping into a lake. That GIF was captioned with "I must go, my people need me." Which I took to mean he had another after hours emergency call.

One thing I've learned in our brief acquaintance is that Tate works long hours. He's devoted to his business, to where he often works through his lunches. And his clients sometimes get too demanding with him. It sounds stressful.

Stressful enough to make me long to pamper him with warm bubble baths before bed and homemade meals to fill his belly. If he was my boy, I'd pack him a lunch, so he'd stop skipping food. I want to make his life easier and I want to see his cares drift away while he colors, or watches cartoons or has a playdate with his friends.

I can picture him playing fetch with Q or roughhousing with Monty. And I want to be a part of his life so that I get to see those special moments. I might even get to be a part of them. But for now, we're just texting back and forth and making vague plans to hang out at Adventures.

Tate offered to bring me as his visitor last Friday night. Unfortunately, I had to back out after I got called in to do some last-minute retakes on a project that was supposed to be finished weeks ago. I was lucky there was some free studio time on short notice, so I had to take what I got. I'm just glad he believed me when I told him it was a work emergency instead of assuming I was blowing him off.

Weeks of texting have led to us having something of a routine. He's been open about letting me daddy him a little this way. He even calls me daddy consistently when we chat before bed. It's not the same as playing in person, but it soothes something in me that's been missing for a long time.

My first morning in the new place starts out wonderful. I wake up to the aroma of my automatic coffee maker having done its job and a message from Tate on my phone. He sent me a GIF of a cartoon character diving into a large mug of coffee. Smiling, I send him a brief text.

Rory: Good morning. Here I was thinking you might need a wake-up call after how late you were working last night. ;)

Tate: I'm up. :)

Rory: Good boy. You deserve a reward.

Tate replies with a mug emoji and a question mark.

Rory: Whatever you want. We should get coffee together for real some time. But for now, digital will have to do.

I send him a selfie of my first sip of coffee from my brand new oversized coffee mug. He replies in kind. The picture of him sitting in his work van, wearing his dark blue work coveralls with a beat up metal travel mug in his work-roughened hand is irrationally sexy. His expression, eyes heavy-lidded and barely parted lips moist from his cup, makes my libido take notice. I palm myself through my pajama pants, euphoric at the weight of my dick in my palm.

As I rub my hand over my bulge, I can't help thinking of my vague promise to play with Tate and his friends sometime soon at Adventures. Reluctantly, I stop touching myself and make toast. If I had someone to cook for, I might make something to go with the toast, but this will tide me over until lunch. A brief fantasy of sharing breakfast with Tate as my boy flits through my thoughts.

I can picture his big rough hands wrapped around a warm bottle. Would he take his coffee in a bottle? Or a sippy cup? Or would he want something more kid friendly in that headspace? Is he little in the mornings? Thinking of him in my home first thing in the morning makes me smile. Does he ever wear a diaper? I want to know those things about him.

I need to make time for the tour of the club Martin offered me so I can start the membership process at Adventures. Now that I have a permanent address, I need to bump contacting Martin up my priority list. Part of me wants to invite Tate over to play, but I got the impression he'd be more comfortable playing in a neutral location, like the club. At least for our first play date.

Well, no time like the present to get in touch. I pull up my email client and dig through my wallet for the card Martin gave me to message him about joining. When I hit send, I get an out of office auto-reply that the club is closed except to reserve private rooms until further notice.

Rory: Oh, and just FYI, I'm messaging Martin. Any idea why he'd be out of his office?

Tate: Call me?

Rory: Sure.

I'm used to Tate's preference for avoiding longer conversations via text, so I dial his number and press the phone to my ear.

"Hi, Daddy." That word in Tate's growly morning voice is one of the hottest things ever. I want to hear it in person. There are traffic sounds coming through the line, though, which has me on alert.

"Hello, Tate. You aren't driving, are you?"

"I've got my bluetooth headset and I'm just about to leave for my first call. Also, I'm rolling my eyes at you. Can't turn off Daddy mode, huh?" he teases.

"Not when it comes to my boy's safety." I agree.

"And am I your boy?" His tone is light, but there's an underlying insecurity to the words.

"If you get to call me daddy, then I get to claim you as my boy. Unless you aren't ready for that yet?" I check. We mostly stick to the daddy thing during our bedtime phone calls, where I read him a story.

"I am. I like the way you take care of me. It just feels weird, since we haven't really gotten to play in person yet. You know?"

"I get that. And I'd like to remedy the situation as soon as possible. Hence getting set up to come to the club."

"Yeah." Tate groans. "About that..."

"Oh no. Did you ask me to call because there's something wrong? Did something happen to Martin or the club?"

"Martin is fine. The club, on the other hand...let's just say that's where I was last night. It's not looking like we'll be able to play there for at least several months."

"Oh. Fiddlesticks. That puts a damper on our plans, doesn't it?" I ask. Hopefully, he'll be open to figuring out an alternative venue for us to get together in person again now that our plan to play on neutral ground at the club is out the window.

"Yeah. I don't really want to wait for Martin to reopen. I mean, we've already fucked, so it *shouldn't* be a big deal for me to come over again, right?"

"No shoulds about you feeling safe, little one. I'm willing to do whatever makes you comfortable."

"You make me comfortable. But since you asked, Kylee is having a play party for the gang from the club next week. How about you come with me?"

"Would Kylee be alright with you inviting me along?"

"Yeah, of course. She'd probably prefer it to me playing with a relative stranger in private for the first time. She can be a total momma bear with us. We have a deal where she takes care of us. My friends and me, I mean."

"If Kylee and Q are alright with it, then I would love to join you at their party. They both seem like great friends."

"Cool, they are pretty great. I'll tell them to expect you." Tate enthuses, and I can picture his excited smile, even though I've only known him a short while. He gets more animated when he lets himself sink into little space and embrace his interests. It's one trait I like about him.

We flesh out our plans more before Tate gets to his first scheduled job for the day. After we exchange goodbyes, I get myself ready to head to work early so I can run some errands before my recording time. I have some ideas for when I eventually get to have Tate visit in person, and I want everything to be perfect for my boy when the time comes. And that means tracking down a few special surprises for him for when he's

ready to come to my place.

CHAPTER 9

Rory

Shortly after Tate invites me to their play party, Q sends me an excited DM about what to expect. Kylee messages me the house rules they have for all their guests. It's fairly standard, and the confirmation that both hosts are fine with Tate inviting me makes me relax about going. I'm a little nervous about dipping a toe back into the caretaker role with an audience, but I'm glad that Tate has a community that looks out for him. They don't know me, but they're willing to give me a chance.

We continue to chat every night leading up to the party, and I can tell Tate is as excited about going as I am. We're both counting down the days. When the morning finally arrives, I have a hard time focusing on work. Tate sends me excited GIFs all day and I send back similar pictures. He calls me when I send him a reminder to take his lunch break in the form of a picture of Garfield attacking a pan of lasagna.

"Hey," Tate greets me when I answer his call. "I don't have time to have a sit down meal like that. I've got big plans tonight, so I need to finish today's jobs in time to grab a shower and change."

"Oh, yeah? Is there anything special *I* should wear?"

"Nah, your regular clothes are fine. No one there will care. I mean, some folks wear harnesses and stuff under their street clothes, but there's no actual dress code. Or fetish wear requirement. Unless you want to?"

"Hm, I'm not exactly into leather or anything. What are you

wearing?"

"Probably something cozy."

"Like a onesie pajama?"

"Is that something you want to see?"

"Yeah." I lick my lips. "Bet your little boy pajamas are nice and soft, huh? It would be cozy to curl up with you in a chair, rock you and read you stories."

Tate groans. "That sounds nice."

"It does. I don't suppose Q and Kylee have a nice big rocking chair for us to borrow?"

"Nope, they have a cozy recliner and a big sectional in the play area, though. And bean bag chairs, so we can find a spot to cuddle."

"What else do you want to do?" I ask.

"Probably play with the pups. Q has some puppy friends. I think this is their usual puppy mosh night, but there was a scheduling issue so they are hosting. Anyway, they invited the littles from the club to join since Adventures is closed and the pups like to play with us."

"So, should I be ready to play fetch and scratch puppy ears?"

"Yeah, probably. We'll get to play too. Just, you know, I might also wrestle around with Q."

"Sounds fun."

"It is. Q will almost definitely offer to blow you. They weren't lying when they said they like to give head and that Kylee likes to indulge them. Um, so, yeah, and Q might not be the only one having sex."

"They mentioned that." I rub at my chin, unsure how much I actually want to engage in anything sexual in public. I don't have a problem with watching, but it's never really been my thing.

"Are you interested?" Tate asks. The note of vulnerability in his voice gives me hope that he's thought of me since our night together, too.

"In Q? Not really. I like them, but I don't want to fuck them."

"You don't?" Tate sounds relieved about that, but that could be wishful thinking on my part. I haven't been able to get him out of my head since that first night together and that's only intensified since we exchanged numbers at the munch.

"No. I've been talking with this boy I'm really interested in and I don't want to have sex with anyone else. Not even oral." I lay my cards on the table for him.

"You don't?" Tate sounds surprised at the admission.

"Nope. I'm a bit of a one person sort of person. Not that I have an issue with Q and Kylee doing what works for them. Just, that wouldn't work for me."

"You mean me, right?" Tate asks.

"Yeah, Tate, I mean you." I nod, even though he can't see me through the phone. "You're the one I want."

"Good. I want you, too. But you should know that I hardly ever have sex when I'm little. Oral or otherwise. And I kind of want to take things slow with you."

"I can go slow." I'm not sure how to feel about his admission, but it sounds like it's not about me. So I can either respect his boundaries or stop pursuing him. That's a no-brainer. I already know Tate is worth waiting for. "No pressure, but can you elaborate on what you mean? Like when you say usually, does that mean there are circumstances where you would have sex with your daddy or caretaker?"

"I might? I don't play that way in public. At all. But in private, with someone I'm in a serious relationship with, it's different. Last time I got that close to someone, it was a disaster for me."

"I'm sorry. Do you want to tell me more about it?" I figure he wouldn't have brought his ex up if he didn't want to talk about whatever happened.

"It's nothing too terrible. I was just young and foolish. Gary was older, and he swept me off my feet. I ended up moving in too soon and it caused problems. It's why Luke ended up buying my uncle's place instead of me. I was living with Gary at the time and he didn't think I should take on debt to buy my uncle out. It almost cost me buying into the business because Gary wanted me to let him take care of me financially and it was…not healthy for me."

"Sorry to hear that, Tate. I take it you don't want your daddy to handle your finances then?" I try not to read too much into what he said and picture horrific scenarios with this Gary cast as a villain. Tate says it was just a poor fit, so I'll have to take him at his word. Still, the idea of a daddy trying to sabotage Tate's professional ambitions leaves a sour taste in my mouth.

"Nope. With the business, I'm the one in charge. I think it boiled down to him being embarrassed that I work with my hands, but now that's a hard limit for me. I need control of my professional life. Anyway, all that to say, it might take me a while to get to where I can share sexual intimacy with you again if we're together."

"I'd never want to stifle you from reaching your goals, financial or otherwise, Tate."

"I know. And I know you think my coveralls are sexy," Tate teases me.

"Guilty." I chuckle.

"So," Tate draws out the word, his worry palpable. "Is the no sex for now a deal-breaker, or do you still want to keep seeing me?"

"It's not a deal-breaker. But, so we're on the same page, do you want to work toward a committed relationship where you might eventually want sex with me?" I ask. "Seriously, no pressure either way."

"I mean, that's the point of dating, right?" Tate forces a half-hearted laugh.

"It doesn't have to be." I assure him. "We could just be playing together. Or taking sex slow could mean keeping the sex and age play parts of our relationship separate, or any number of things. That's why I'm asking what you want out of this."

"I want to find a forever daddy to play with and share my life with." He says with confidence. "And eventually, in an ideal world, that would include sex."

"That sounds perfect to me. So, we're agreed on not having sex tonight, or for a while?" I summarize for him.

"Yeah." Tate says wistfully. Almost like a part of him regrets the boundary is necessary. But he set it and I won't push him for anything he isn't ready for. "Definitely not with other people. I enjoy snuggles, but I don't want it to be sexual. Not for now."

"But you want to date me?"

"Yeah."

"And keep calling me Daddy?" I try not to come across as overeager, but I want that with him.

"Yeah, if that's okay?"

"Of course. I'd love to be your daddy. For a scene, or whenever we get together, whatever you're comfortable with. Is there something you'd want me to call you when you're little? I heard Monty calling you Tatey-Tot."

He chuckles. "Yeah, that's an old family nickname. They also call me Tater-Tot. Tate doesn't exactly lend itself to shortening."

"Hm, at the risk of revealing myself as a total nerd, how about if I call you precious?"

"I don't follow."

"Like the Gollum scene from LOTR: 'What's taters, precious?'" I pitch my voice like the character from the movie. Tate is silent for a beat and I'm worried I overstepped, but then he busts up laughing.

"Dang, you're good at that. So, you want to call me precious because of a line from a movie about a monster who has an unhealthy obsession?" He sounds amused.

"And because if you agree to be my little boy, you'd be precious to me?" I try to sound casual about it, but having a little to take care of is worth treasuring. Silliness aside.

"Ha, smooth answer. Yeah, you can call me that. Or Tate, or whatever else fits when we're in the moment. You're really okay being my daddy without sex being part of it?"

"Sure. Whatever you need, I wouldn't want to do anything you aren't comfortable with. Just to be clear, if we're dating, does that mean we might get together for sex outside of your little time? Or is that also a no?"

"I don't know. Probably eventually? I don't want to tell you sex is totally off the table, because our night together was hot. But I almost never have sex with people that I'm playing with because it makes things messy. Emotionally. For me. Is that a deal-breaker?"

"Not at all. I never want to make you uncomfortable. At least, not in a bad way." I try to lighten the mood and Tate rewards my joke with a slight chuckle. "I'm glad you're sharing your boundaries with me. Now, you need to get yourself something to eat, so I won't keep you on the phone."

"I *might* have time to grab a burrito or something on my way to my next job, since you're so insistent." Tate's tone is more teasing than exasperated, despite his words.

"Good, I don't want to nag, but you shouldn't go all day without eating."

"Yes, Daddy, I know." Tate drawls and damn, does that word feel perfect coming from him. A jolt of fitting just right with another person. "I'll even send you proof, if it makes you happy."

"That would make Daddy very happy. Oh, before I forget, are you planning to take the bus to Kylee and Quent's place?" I ask, not quite ready to say goodbye, even though we both need to get back to our jobs.

"Nope, driving." Tate replies.

"Can I pick you up?"

"Are you sure you don't mind?"

"Yeah, you can be my navigator, since you know where we're going and where the best parking is. And we're going together, so it would be nice to, you know, go together."

"Yeah. Okay, I'll text you my address, so you'll have it for the GPS." Tate agrees.

"Sounds good. See you tonight, precious."

"See you soon, Daddy."

"And don't forget to text me a pic of my boy with his big tasty burrito."

He snorts before hanging up. About fifteen minutes later, he sends me a selfie with his mouth wrapped around a burrito as thick as his forearm. Damn. He's hot as fuck and I just agreed to take it slow with him. From the way he talked about keeping sex and playtime separate, it will be a long while before I get to see those gorgeous lips wrapped around my cock. Heck, it might never happen, even if we are dating. Am I really okay with that?

Yeah. I think I am. I don't need to have sex to be happy. Most of my recent fantasies star moments that are utterly G-rated. What I want more than anything is someone who will let me take care of them. No, not just let me, someone who will love those tender gestures as much as I do.

I want to cuddle my little one in my arms as they fall asleep watching cartoons. I want to give my boy a bath. Or watch him lose himself in play. Take care of Tate when he's vulnerable. Whether that means cleaning him up in the bathtub, feeding him, or even changing his diapers.

Tate might not be ready to have sex with me again anytime soon, but he sounds open to doing the things I really want with a partner. And sure, it's a little weird that he was more fine sleeping with a stranger than a guy he's dating, but he has his reasons. Reasons I hope we can build enough trust to move past someday, when he's ready. And if he's never ready, I meant what I said. It's enough to have a little to dote upon. I'm looking forward to tonight.

CHAPTER 10

Tate

Rory picks me up at my place after work. It's a bit awkward to see him in person after weeks of calling each other and texting. Strange to see him outside our usual context of a video chat for him to read me a story and virtually tuck me into bed.

"Hi, Daddy." I greet him with a bashful wave as I get into the car, immediately overthinking whether I should call him that here. Daddy beams at the title, even brighter than when I say it over a video chat. So, I'm pretty sure I should keep calling him that. It feels right, and that helps me to relax around him. We might not have spent much in person time together, but we talk daily. It seems like I've known him much longer than a scant month.

We make small talk on the drive to Q's place. I vent to him about my latest difficult clients and he tells me about a scheduling conflict that means he'll be working this weekend to make a deadline. So much for asking to hang out again on Saturday, like I'd hoped we might if tonight goes well.

Still, I enjoy talking to him. It's the sort of day-to-day conversation that I'd have with my friends. Sharing the less than enthralling details of my life, and even though it's totally mundane, I like how he listens with interest and asks me questions. And it doesn't escape my notice that he keeps stealing hungry glances at me.

We aren't the first to arrive at Q's place, so we have to

park down the street. At least they live in a residential part of Westminster with plenty of free on-street parking. Rory offers me his hand when we get out and I take it. There's nothing obviously Daddyish about the gesture. But it makes me feel small and cared for that he twines our fingers together and puts himself between me and traffic as we walk along the sidewalk.

I swing our joined hands between us and he gives me an indulgent smile, like he can tell I'm already slipping into a younger headspace. Hope is the one to answer when I knock. Makes sense. Kylee likes to be present when people are playing in her space, so she's probably downstairs supervising.

"Come on in. Kylee and Q are down in the play area. Angel is down there playing with the puppies, or they'd be here with me on door duty. You know the drill." Hope echoes my thoughts as she gestures to the neatly arranged shoes that the other guests have left on the rack by the door. Q must have stashed the shoes that normally live there somewhere else for the night. If I know my friend, they're probably dumped in a pile in Q and Kylee's closet to deal with later. I add my shoes to an empty spot on the rack.

Hope takes the hoodie I wore over to cover the top half of my onesie when I shrug out of it while Daddy is still fussing with his laces. I don't wear my little stuff where just anyone can see it and judge me. She hangs my hoodie on an empty hook. I tug the top part of the outfit straight.

Rory stands, sets his shoes next to mine on the rack, and turns to face me. "Ready?" He stares at the fuzzy applique penguin on my onesie.

"What?" I glance down, self-consciously at the bird.

"Nothing. You look good." He licks his lips and I offer him a tentative smile, hoping he meant what he said about taking things slow when we spoke earlier. I like him, but I still don't want to get in over my head.

"Thanks. You ready?" I reach for his hand and he lets me take it.

"Yep." He agrees. Permission granted, I haul my daddy toward the door to the basement. Rory lets me drag him along with me, calling back to Hope, "Nice to see you again."

"Someone is eager to play," she teases. "I'm sure we'll chat more later." Hope waves after us. And as much as it might be polite to linger for him to make friends with the other bigs I'm friends with, she's right that I'm excited to see what Rory is like as a daddy.

The basement door is open and I lead the way down the wide stairs to Q's play area. It's pretty clear they designed the space with Q's preferences in mind. One corner looks like a typical finished basement with plush carpet and a nice couch and a matching armchair. The wall next to it is floor to ceiling shelves of Quent's pup toys and gear.

The large open play area with the gymnastic style mats and a puppy agility course set up on it looks smaller when it's crowded with Q's pup friends. Several handlers I don't know well are standing off to the sides while their pups play together. I could probably match up most of them to their pups from the way their eyes track the play.

I don't bother those pups, instead I go over to join Connor. He's standing near the couch throwing a toy for Q and a pup with no collar and no handler in sight. Jax is watching them play with that same avid interest I recognize from the pup handlers. Connor and the two pups seem oblivious to their appreciative audience. I consider waving, but when Jax notices me observing him, he tips back his bottle of water for a sip and turns to talk to the pup handler beside him.

"Hey, Tate." Connor grins at me and Daddy. "Hey, it was Rory, right?"

"Yep, good to see you again, Connor." Rory waves a greeting at my friend.

"Hey, Con. Hey, Q." I pull Connor into a quick side hug. At the mention of their name, Q turns and greets me with a joyful bark and a tail wag. I can just see their tongue lolling out in a doggy grin under the leather pup hood.

The uncollared pup seems shy when Rory and I get close, but they follow Q over to nose at me. I crouch to their level and offer a hand for each pup to sniff. The new pup crouches at a wary distance, so I stay where I am and wait to see if they approach.

Q ambles up to me and nudges their face into my lap in a demand for affection. They paw at me with happy little barks. I give my friend scritches, laughing when they lick my nose, then push them away to greet the new pup.

"Hey, Q, say hi to Daddy Rory while I say hi to your new friend." I reach for the new pup again and they come tentatively toward me, nosing at my hand and then leaning closer to let me scratch them too. Q nuzzles into Rory's knee and Daddy ruffles their ears.

"Hey there, Q, are you a good little pup?" Daddy pets them. I glance over, not sure how I should feel about my date paying attention to someone else. It might be weird to some people, but I enjoy watching him be sweet and affectionate with my friend. Q sits and wags their tail while Daddy lavishes attention and ear rubs on them.

"Who is this?" I ask as the new pup rests their chin on my knee. That seems like an invitation to fuss with the pup's pointy ears and pet their soft hair.

"That's Daisy." Con scooches over to us and waves the floppy rope toy he was throwing for the two pups toward the pup in question. "She's new to puppy play, but she's a very good girl, aren't you, Daisy?"

Daisy turns to Con and wriggles, her floppy tail wagging behind her. Q catches sight of the still waving toy, and pounces toward it with a playful yip.

"Want to play fetch some more?" Con asks, moving the toy just out of reach. Q bows down, butt waggling in the air like a bio pup eager to play. They bark an affirmative. Laughing, Con throws the toy. Q runs off after it.

Daisy scrabbles away from me to chase them. The two pups scuffle over the toy briefly before Daisy grabs one end and Q grabs the other. They both bring it back for Con to throw again. I scoot closer to Con and we both shower the pups with praise and pats for bringing us the toy. Con lets me take the next throw. Daddy stays with us for a few rounds of fetch, then he taps my shoulder to get my attention.

"You keep playing. Daddy's going to go thank Miss Kylee for inviting us tonight, okay?" Rory gestures to where Kylee is standing nearby, watching us play with her pup. I wave at her and she waves back with a smile.

"Okay, Daddy." I grin up at him. Daddy ruffles my hair and goes over to Kylee. Con throws the toy, then nudges me in the ribs as both pups tear off after it again.

"Daddy?" Con cuts his eyes toward Rory.

"For tonight anyway." I shrug like it's no big deal.

"You like him."

I pick at the carpet. "It's nothing. This is our first time actually playing. But we've been talking since the munch."

"Texting or actually talking?" Con arches a brow at me.

"Both. And video chats for bedtime." I can't help smiling at the memory of Daddy reading to me every night.

"Aw, so he's not a big meanie who makes you text him 'like any other person under thirty'?" Con puts exaggerated air quotes around the last part because it's crap I've heard from way too many potential dates and he knows how much it bugs me.

"Rude." I elbow Con. "Nope. He's really respectful. And he reminds me to take my lunch break and reads me bedtime stories."

"OMG, you've got a telephone Daddy to do bedtime with you? Jealous!" Con fake pouts.

"Sorry."

"Don't be." Con waves off my concern. "I can want what you have and still be happy that you have it. So, does he like the same kinds of play as you?"

"I'm not sure, but I guess that's the point of playing together, to see. Right?"

"Yep."

"Anyway." I shrug and try to change the subject. "It's nothing serious."

"Fair enough." Con lets me get away with avoiding further discussion. "Have you seen Monty yet?"

"He might be late tonight. I spoke to him earlier to see if he still wanted a ride since I drove over here with Rory. He said he was running behind schedule. He's grabbing a bus." I relay the information.

What Monty actually said was that he was sitting staring at his closet instead of deciding what to wear because his work day sucked out all his energy. Now that he's home, his brain glitched on him so he needs time to decompress before coming out. He still plans to make it to the party as soon as he gets dressed. That's all more detail than he'd want to tell everyone here, so I paraphrase. It's enough for Con to know Monty will be here later.

"Ah. Cool. So, are we the only boys here so far?" Con asks as he takes the toy from Daisy and throws it again.

"Maybe? Not the only littles, at least. Angel's here." I point toward where I saw them earlier.

"Oh, yeah?" Con looks around for the other little, then grins when he sees them chatting with one of the pup handlers across the room. The handler is showing off their pup's tricks. Con catches Angel's eye and waves.

I wave, too. We're not close outside kinky get-togethers, but we play together a lot since we're in the same circles. Angel is one of Luke's go to models when my brother does rope demos. They return the greeting with a smile before turning their attention back to the pup doing a spin at their feet.

"I've been meaning to check in and see how Bethany is holding up with the broken arm." Con mentions Hope and Angel's pre-teen daughter.

"Right." It's my turn to throw the rope for the pups, as Q makes clear by shoving it against my belly. I pat their head and toss the toy. "Poor kid. I forgot to ask Hope how she's doing."

"Last I heard, she doesn't need surgery, just a couple months in a cast." Of course, Con would think to ask. He has too many siblings and niblings for me to keep them all straight, and he likes kids.

"Craptastic way to spend a summer." I commiserate.

"Yep. Marietta was a terror the summer that she sprained her ankle and had to miss out on her camps." Con pauses for another throw. Then he changes the subject with a pointed glance toward the other people playing around us. "So, you're here to play with your new daddy, right?"

"Yeah." I nod.

"So, like, go play with him." He nudges my shoulder. "I can keep the pups busy."

That's when Q deposits their slobbery toy in my lap again. I pat their head and pretend to throw it. Which gets Daisy to run a few steps before realizing it was a trick. Q gives me a disgusted look and a huffy bark. They paw at my leg impatiently. Their body language couldn't be a clearer prompt that the stupid human should just throw the toy already.

"Fine, have it your way." I toss the toy up into the air. Q jumps for it and makes an impressive midair catch.

"Good pup," Con praises them. Q wags their tail and gives me a dismissive glance before offering their toy to Con. They lean in to lick his chin before dancing back a few steps to wait for the next throw. Con obliges. "Go on, Tate." Con shoos me away.

I scan the room for Rory. I don't really want to throw the toy anymore. Honestly, I'd rather snuggle on Daddy's lap and watch the puppies running around and being silly. I yawn and decide to fuck self-consciousness; I want to be little tonight. Even if the larger than I expected crowd in Q's basement has me feeling out of sorts, I want to play. If I act little, the headspace will usually come to me. So I crawl over to the couch where I spot Daddy sitting and chatting with Jax.

Daddy Rory looks busy, but he holds out his hands for me. I reach up to him and he lifts me up to plop me on his lap, bouncing me on his knee. Daddy doesn't miss a beat in his conversation. I pop my thumb into my mouth, slouch to rest my head on Daddy's shoulder and just bask in him. I've daydreamed of a life where snuggles like this could be my daily reality.

Rory is so perfect for me. I've craved a daddy like him for so long. Someone who is so used to holding me and offering me silent comfort that he doesn't blink at me needing him in the middle of a party. Or interrupting a conversation with that need.

This is what I want. More to the point, it's a thing I didn't fully realize I wanted until Rory showed it to me just now. I snuggle closer and he bounces his knee a bit, rocking me gently.

"Is this your boy?" Jax asks.

"Yes, Tate, say hi to Jackson."

I giggle because I know Jax, and he isn't one for using full names. "Hi, Mx. Jax," I slur the words around my thumb. Jax ruffles my hair.

"Hello little Tate. Are you having fun tonight?"

"Uh, huh." I nod.

"Your daddy was telling me he's new to the city, and he met Kylee and Q at a munch last month. It's too bad Adventures had to close, huh? The club makes it easier to meet people and get acquainted on neutral ground."

"Yeah." I nod, still not removing my thumb from my mouth. Daddy pats my leg and continues to rock me gently.

"We were going to meet up there for our first playdate, so it worked out nicely for us that Q and Kylee were kind enough to extend an invitation." Rory adds.

"Don't be silly, Daddy." I take my thumb out to say the rest. Getting drawn into conversation is pulling me away from the headspace I was seeking with the habit, anyway. "Q always invites me to their parties. Unless it's a puppy mosh."

"Is that right?" Daddy asks.

"Yeah." I nod. "There's so many more puppies than I expected here tonight. Quent said their usual pup mosh venue double booked their night this month, so Miss Kylee agreed to invite all their pup friends and everyone from Adventures. It's been a rough month for all their social circles, I guess."

"You mentioned that in the car earlier, precious. Are you

having a hard time being little with the crowd?"

I nod. His arms around me and the little name he chose just for me help me feel smaller, though.

"Why don't we find some toys for you to play with?" Daddy murmurs near my ear. It tickles, so I scrunch my neck and nod, then squirm off his lap before he can tickle me anymore.

"Okay, Daddy. Let's go!" I know where Kylee keeps the good toys for when littles visit. I scoot along the floor to the cabinet where they're tucked away on the bottom shelf of the unit holding all Q's puppy gear.

The toys are all thrown together in a large bin that I drag onto the floor, unprompted. Daddy follows behind me. I peer inside at the familiar hodgepodge of toys. Blocks, cars, a couple of action figures, some dolls, and accessories, along with a few well-worn picture books. One of Q's chewy toys is mixed in with everything else and I pluck that out to set it aside for them.

"Are you allowed to go through Q's things without permission?" Daddy asks as I grab the entire bin.

"Yep, Miss Kylee got all this stuff for us to play with, she says. C'mon and play, Daddy." I shove the toy bin toward him and he takes it from me, then lets me drag him to an out of the way corner near a bean bag chair. I plop down onto the carpet, then scramble onto my knees beside the chair and gesture for Daddy to join me. He sits more carefully and offers me the bin of toys.

"What are we playing with first?" Daddy pulls out a book with a puppy on the cover.

I pout. "Stories are for bedtime. It's not bedtime."

"Stories can be all the time." Daddy corrects me, but he sets aside the book. "Okay, what would you like to play?"

"Race cars." I grab the box from him and pull out a fistful of blocks. Daddy looks confused, so I explain. "First, we gotta build a racetrack, and then you race me. It's gotta be epic and big and use all the blocks."

"I see."

"And when I win, you can give me kisses." I tap my cheek in emphasis, so he'll know where to kiss me.

"Oh, I can, can I? And what if Daddy wins?"

"Then I'll give you kisses." I lean in to peck his cheek in demonstration.

"Kisses, huh?" Daddy smiles at me, his eyes on my mouth.

"Yep. On the cheek." I point to my cheek again, to be sure he gets the rules.

"Ok then." Daddy grins at me and rubs his hands together like he's excited to start. "Let's build this epic racetrack."

Daddy helps sort out all the blocks for me while I place them along the race course. Monty and Con join us at some point. I'm glad Monty mustered up the energy to get here, even when he acts all bossy about how to finish the track and who gets what car. I'm not sure I want to share my daddy time, even with my closest friends. But we *are* at a party and Daddy welcomed them into our game, so I don't complain. Still, it's frustrating that my friends joining the game messes up my plans for kisses.

When the track is complete, Monty claims a bright green car. Daddy grabs the blue one and drives it around in front of me. He makes engine noises and rolls it gently along one of my arms before he holds it out to me. His car noises make me laugh, so I push it back to him. "You drive that one, Daddy."

Con chooses the dragon figure to use instead of a car, so that means I can pick pretty much any toy still in the box. Digging through the toys, I bypass the silver car with cool fire decals in favor of a sparkly pink pony.

"I'll win with my trusty pony, Noodle." I hold the pony aloft.

Con snorts. "Not if Darkness the dragon eats you first." He has his dragon try to bite Noodle in the neck, but I deflect him with my other hand.

"Nope, Noodle has a magic shield, so your stinky Darkness can't get close enough to eat me. Also, if you keep trying, I'm totally going to cast magic missile at Darkness."

Monty and Con both crack up at that. "Just for that, I won't devour you today, pony." Con sets his dragon down on the starting line.

I glance over at Daddy for a reaction. He looks bemused at our silliness, but doesn't seem to get the joke. So, okay, not into tabletop nerd memes. That's fine. Monty offers me a fist bump.

"Daddy, will you do the ready, set, go?" I ask. He does and we all move our racers along the track. Monty copies Daddy's car sounds and Con makes a few dinosaur shrieks. I do a half-hearted clip-clop for a bit, but then I get too into actually trying to win to keep it up.

It's all fun and games until Darkness takes flight on the second lap. Con hovers the toy just high enough to get past Monty's car when it cuts him off every time he tries to pass.

"Hey! No fair." Monty bats the toy out of Con's hand. "You're cheating."

"Am not!" Con shoves at Monty and retrieves the dragon. "Dragons have wings. Why wouldn't they fly when they race? You aren't calling Tate a cheater for using his hooves instead of wheels!"

"Tate isn't leaving the ground." Monty grumbles.

Con rolls his eyes. "Duh, because horses *can't* fly."

"Magic sparkling unicorns can, though. So I *could* fly, if I wanted." I interject. "But I just wanted to race. And you two are ruining it." I glower at them both.

Monty and Con both open their mouths to reply, but Daddy clears his throat in that way bigs do when you know you're going to get in trouble. That gets all three of us to turn toward him. I hunch my shoulders, instantly aware that this is my first time playing with him, my little side on full display. A fight with my friends is hardly what I wanted him to see.

"Hey, now, let's not fight." Daddy says. "What would make the race seem more fair to you, Monty?"

"Not having anything that can fly." Monty insists. "They have to stay on the track."

"And Connor?"

"He uses Con when he's little, Daddy." I interrupt, even though I don't want to draw anymore negative attention. It's what Con prefers, and he's already surpassed his lifetime quota for having to correct people about what to call him. So if I can help, even if it's just about his little nickname, I will. Con shoots me a thankful smile.

"I'm sorry, is it okay if I call you Con?" Daddy corrects himself.

"Yep!" Con nods. "What should we call you?"

"What do you want to call me?" Daddy asks.

"You came with Tate, so does that make you Tate's Daddy?" Con guesses. The words fill me with a radiating warmth. I like them knowing Rory is mine.

"You can call me that, or Rory," Daddy suggests.

"Okay. Thanks, Tate's Daddy. Maybe Tate and I can race in the air above the track separate from you and Monty racing the cars on the track?" Con demonstrates his suggestion with his dragon hovering over the track.

"What do you think of that, Monty?" Daddy asks.

Monty bites his lip skeptically, but he nods.

"So can we all agree it would be fair if the two cars race and then the flying animals race separately at the same time?" Daddy repeats the compromise.

"Yes." Monty and Con agree.

"Precious?" Daddy looks right at me.

"Oh, yeah. That sounds fair, Daddy." I flash him a tentative smile. He must not be mad about refereeing a silly squabble if he's still calling me that.

"Good. Let's start a new race then." Daddy returns his car to the start of the track, Monty joins him. Con and I hover our racers above the track and we start over.

We do a few races. Angel wanders over to join us before the third race. They choose the silver car I usually like and we zoom around the track several more times.

Each of us has at least one win under our belts before Monty loses interest and wanders away to see who among the bigs is available to play with him. Or more to the point, to find someone he can entice into spanking him. He makes a half-hearted offer to help clean up first, but he's already standing and scanning the room for the next thing he wants to do. I'm not ready to stop my game with Daddy yet, so I wave Monty away. "We'll clean up when we're done. Go have fun."

We play with the racing track for a while longer before Angel asks if we can build towers with the blocks instead. We do that for a while, playing with the action figures.

Daddy joins right in with the game. He has the best silly voices for the figures I press into his hands. All three of us laugh and Con and Angel hand him toys, too, asking him to do more characters for them. There's a Sparkles figure, because of course Q has all the pup merch they can get, and Angel gives me a gleeful look when Daddy does the real Sparkles voice. It gives me a weird rush of pride to tell them that my daddy sounds like Sparkles because he *is* Sparkles. Even if Daddy corrects me about the dog actor and says he just does the voice.

We play until Hope finishes greeting new arrivals upstairs and comes to collect Angel for a diaper change. Con and I knock down our tower and start a new one, but I'm kind of over the blocks and needing to share my daddy. Rory came here with me tonight, and it's fun to play with other littles, but this might be my only chance to play with him for a while. I want to make the most of it.

I look around for the pup Con was playing with earlier. There's no sign of Daisy, but Jax catches my eye. He seems to notice that Con is an unintentional third wheel, so he comes over and squats down beside us.

"Hey, Conman! How would you like it if I read you a storybook?"

"Can you read to Darkness, too?" Con holds up the dragon toy.

"Sure thing, little dude. Come on, let's pick out a book and let Tate and his daddy finish their game, okay?"

"Oh." Con flashes me an apologetic look, like it's just now dawning on him I might have wanted to play with Rory alone. "Yeah, sorry, Tate and Tate's Daddy. Want help to tidy the blocks, or are you still playing?"

"Not a problem, the more the merrier." Daddy assures Con. "Tate, did you want to race again?"

"No." I toss a fistful of blocks back into the bin. Con helps, then gives me a big hug around the neck.

"Sorry," Con mumbles into my ear.

"It's okay," I grumble back. It's hard to stay mad when I enjoy playing together. I just want one-on-one time with Daddy, too. As much as that's possible with so many people gathered here today. Maybe that's selfish, but I've been wanting to meet up with Rory in person again for weeks now, and I intend to make the most of tonight.

Con squeezes me again. Then he takes his time selecting a stack of books from the box for Jax to read to him. Con offers each of his selections to Jax one at a time. As if he's sure Jackson will change his mind about his offer to read together at any second. He won't. He's another person I know mostly through Luke, but my brother isn't friendly with assholes.

Come to think of it, I'm pretty sure that if it weren't for me feeling awkward about playing in front of my brother, Luke would have come here tonight, too. I really need to work on getting past that hangup. Later. When I don't have a wonderful daddy to worry about impressing enough to snag a second date.

I don't want to worry about anything past tonight, yet, so I focus on Con again. He's adding another book to the stack Jackson is holding. Jax smiles and comments on the pictures, accepting every addition to the growing pile without a hint of whatever negative reaction Con seems to expect. When Con finishes making his selections, Jax leads him over to the cozy armchair in the corner that has its own lamp. Perfect for reading stories.

Jackson is a photographer with a sideline in kinky photos. It's a service Luke often makes use of when he does rope workshops. I've joked about booking him for a kinky boudoir shoot to update my Fet profile, but it's just a joke so far. I don't want to share my little side with the internet at large. Maybe if I had a special person, it could be a fun surprise for them, though.

I can almost imagine gifting Daddy a photo of me in a diaper and nothing else. The thought is absurd. It's way too soon for that level of trust. But I want to have someone in my life I can give that sort of gift to someday. There's no reason that special person *couldn't* be Rory.

Speaking of Rory, he's watching me expectantly, the bin of toys still beside him.

"Sorry, did you say something?" I shake away my daydreams.

"I asked what you wanted to do next?"

"Snuggle?" I suggest with a shrug to downplay how much I want him to hold me like I'm his.

"Sure." Daddy pushes the bin of toys aside and settles back into the squishy bean bag chair. Then he opens his arms to me. I crawl into his lap and let him hold me against his chest. "Want a story while we cuddle?" Daddy offers. I squeeze him tight, so he won't try to get up and grab one of Q's books to read to me. If Con even left any.

"Make one up?" I suggest. "And do the voices?" One of the best parts of Daddy Rory's bedtime stories is the way he makes each character unique.

"Sure, what type of story does my precious boy want?"

I smile at the nickname. "Um, can it be about penguins? With magical fire powers, so they can stay warm?"

"Sure." Daddy cards his fingers through my hair. "I can work with that."

And he does. He weaves an epic story about penguin mages fighting evil leopard seals who try to eat them and steal their magic and their fire. The story lasts a long time, fresh trouble cropping up whenever it seems like the magic penguins are about to win.

Some of Rory's bad guy voices are over the top silly to make me giggle. And it's special because it's all for me. I let myself relax into imagining the scenes he's describing while I suck my thumb and let his story transport me to the magical penguin village.

It's an epic story. And more than the actual words coming out of his mouth, the fact Daddy holds me close and tells it in a soft voice meant just for me makes me feel as warm as the magical fire that keeps the penguin village safe. As long as he's holding me, it's like I could glow just as bright as the magic penguin who saves his colony from the marauding sea lions.

I'm not sure when I fall asleep, but when I wake up, Q is licking my face and Daddy and I are among the last few guests remaining. Kylee crouches down to eye level to talk. She rests her fingertips on my forearm. Her familiar touch helps focus my nap-bleary thoughts. She and Q both show their care with touches, so I'm used to receiving the pair's affection.

"Enough, Q." She gives her pup's collar a gentle tug. Q sits at their mommy's feet and gazes up at her with open adoration. "Did you want to stay the night?" Kylee offers in a soft whisper. She is always looking after us like this. "Clark and Nicholas, some of Q's pup friends, already claimed the guest room, but it's late and the couch is free if you two want to crash here."

I stretch and yawn, not sure how to answer. I've stayed the night with Q and the gang after a play party more than once. But waking up in a platonic tangle of limbs with my besties isn't the same as spending an entire night in a daddy's arms. That sounds amazing, but I don't want to get too attached too fast. Rory is nothing like Gary, but there's still the risk I'll fall too fast again. Miss the signs we don't fit the way I long to.

Daddy saves me from having to decide. He answers before I can find my words. "Thanks, but I can take Tate home."

"You good with that, Tate?" Kylee checks, her hand still on my forearm.

"Yeah," I nod, "Daddy Rory can drive me home. I'll message

you when I'm safely delivered. Thanks for inviting us, Miss Kylee." I'd message Q instead, but they're probably going to crash hard once the last guest leaves, if they played as hard as they usually do when they host a party like this.

"Good, see that you do. And I'm glad you could bring Rory along for your playdate." Kylee taps her fingers on my arm before withdrawing her hand and standing. She smiles at us both. "Drive safe." She directs that last comment at Rory with an unspoken 'or else' heavy in her tone.

"I will," Daddy Rory promises. "Thanks for inviting me tonight. Can I grab some water from the fridge?" Daddy points to the mini fridge where Kylee keeps drinks for when we're playing down here.

"Sure." Kylee nods, then turns to hurry along another lingering guest. Q doesn't follow. They look exhausted and happy. Like a bio-dog after hours running around a dog park. Daddy eases me off his lap and into the cushy bean bag. "Want some water, precious?"

"Yes, please." I smile at him. Daddy kisses my forehead.

"Coming right up, wait here."

Q leans in to lick my cheek again. I ruffle their ears. "You all tuckered out from playing?" I smile at my friend.

Q yips their agreement.

"Me too. I'll call you tomorrow to chat, okay?"

That gets me another yip. Q is too far into pupspace to carry on a conversation right now. I pet them a little longer, then get up to wait for Daddy, and we leave together. Daddy holds my hand as we walk to where we parked. The cool night air goes a long way to clearing out the sleep fog from my nap-hazy thoughts.

Daddy opens the passenger door for me and asks to buckle my

seat belt. It's nothing I'm used to, but the simple gesture makes me feel cared for on a deeper level. Like when he held my hand for the walk up to Q and Kylee's door.

I'm intoxicated by the overwhelming sense that he wants to protect me and take care of me. My smile is sappy as hell when he leans in to kiss my cheek, then shuts my door for me. He holds my hand and we chat about the party and my love of penguins on the drive back to my place.

I suggest playing at his place next time, since I prefer not to invite people into my home. It's a weird mental thing. Ever since Gary, I've had a hard time giving up control in my home. It feels safer to go somewhere else to indulge that part of my nature, like leaving for home is a built in escape hatch, in case I need it.

Bottom line, I'll be more comfortable with Daddy making and enforcing the rules in his space instead of mine. I don't say that, just ask if he'd want to have me over for our next playdate. His enthusiastic agreement banishes all doubt about whether he enjoyed our evening as much as I did. His grin fills my belly with excited butterflies.

When he pulls up to the curb to drop me off, there's a moment when our eyes lock. His longing expression makes it clear we're both fighting the urge to lean over the console and kiss goodnight. The only thing that stops me from going there is the certainty that if I give in to my desire for him, I'll invite him up to my apartment to fuck. It's too soon for that to be a good idea. I'm not about to repeat past mistakes with Rory.

"Night, precious. I'll call you with your bedtime story when I get home, okay?" Daddy takes my hand and squeezes it.

"I wish you could tuck me in for real." I whine as I squeeze his fingers back.

"Soon, but we agreed to take things slow, and it's already late."

"I'm holding you to that soon," I grumble as I unbuckle and get out of his car. Which is silly since I'm the one who insisted on slow.

"That sounds good to me. I had fun tonight, Tate." Daddy doesn't call me out for being fickle.

"Me too. Drive safe." I lean on the car door to blow him a flirty goodbye kiss. He pretends to catch it and press it to his heart. I wave, then trudge to my building. Daddy doesn't pull away until I'm safely inside.

When I have my shoes off and my phone plugged in to charge, I text Kylee a picture of myself in my entryway, smiling from ear to ear. Her reply comes fast. A big thumbs up and a smiley face. I send the picture to Daddy, too. He responds a little while later by calling to read my bedtime story. His soothing voice lulls me to sleep with the fervent hope that tonight was the first of many playdates with him.

CHAPTER 11

Rory

Tate is coming over tonight. We agreed that we both prefer the privacy of home to waiting for another party invite. Plus, the party last week was fun, but I could tell Tate had a hard time finding his little headspace in the crowd.Tate's trust in me, as shown by his agreeing to play at my place, is almost as heady as my excitement at getting to see him as a little again. I practically skip up the steps to my apartment when I get home. There isn't much time for me to prepare before Tate is supposed to arrive.

We spoke earlier, when I called to remind him to have lunch, but that only made me anticipate tonight more. He hits the door buzzer just as I'm throwing our dinner in the oven to bake and putting the finishing touches on his surprises. I buzz him in and go to wait for him by the apartment door.

Fussing with the tissue paper in the gift bag I got for him occupies my hands. Most of what I picked out is simple stuff he's mentioned in passing. I didn't have time to get anything specialized, yet. If tonight goes well, we'll have some shopping to do together, since I am decidedly under-prepared for hosting playtime with a little. Still, I hope Tate likes what I chose for him in my search for fun gifts over the past couple of days since we agreed to play at my place.

He taps on my door. I pull it open for him at the first rap of his knuckles. Tate gives me a startled glance that morphs into a grin as his eyes rove hungrily over my body.

"Hi, Daddy." Tate bounces on his toes. And damn, hearing him call me that is still new and exciting. It sounds even better rolling off his tongue in person than it does on the phone.

"Hi, precious. How are you?" There's a warm glow in my chest at having him here.

"Good." Tate takes off his light jacket, revealing what I thought was a loose pair of sweatpants is actually the bottom of another of his adult rompers. I swallow hard at the sight. I invited him over to play as a little, but I guess part of me wasn't quite ready for what that might entail. Not when he's right here in the privacy of my home. He's so enticing part of me wishes we hadn't decided to take this slow. Then again, I relish the opportunity bond on a deeper level before we jump back into bed. I meant it when I said I'm interested in so much more than sex with Tate.

Still, he is undeniably attractive. The soft baby blue fabric has another of his applique penguins over his heart, leaving little doubt that it's meant to mimic younger clothing. It's a sharp contrast to the utilitarian work coveralls I first saw him wearing. It's weird how such a similar design can connote such opposites. In the one, he's soft and snuggly innocence and in the other he's rough edges and hard working grit. I was drawn to him from the moment we met, but this brings it to another level.

"It's okay if I'm little tonight, right?" He checks when I can't stop staring at the cartoon penguin on his chest. He toes off his shoes and then taps his stockinged toe against the floor while he waits for my response.

"More than. I, uh, got you some presents."

"Oh!" His eyes light up and any self-doubt falls away as he bounces over to take the shiny gift bag from my hands. "Can I open it now?" He levels me with big expectant pleading eyes and I am powerless to refuse him anything in the face of his guileless charm.

"Yeah. Go for it."

Tate tears the tissue paper free and tosses it aside to pull out the penguin stuffie. I found the perfect one at the aquarium gift shop after scouring every toy store near the recording studio, to no avail. He lets out a delighted squee and clutches it to his chest. His joy renders all my efforts to find his favorite animal completely worth my while. "For me?"

"Just for you. Do you like it?" I wasn't sure if he'd want another penguin or something else, but I went with my gut and seeing him hug the toy makes me glad I did.

"Uh, huh. Thank you, Daddy." Tate flings his arms around me to hug me tight. The stuffie presses into my back until he pulls away to examine it again. "What's his name?"

"You can name him anything you want. Is he a boy?"

"Yep." He holds the toy up to his face, so that he's beak to nose with it and considers. "I'm going to call him Spot. Can we play now?" Tate asks.

"Of course, come on in." I lead Tate and Spot into the living room.

"Spot looks like the African penguins at the aquarium. He's gonna be Fuzzy's buddy. Did you know penguins mate for life?"

"Yeah?" I ask, even though I knew that. It seems like a common thing with birds.

"Yep." Tate nods and bounces his new toy along the back of my couch as he sidles closer to me. "And sometimes gay penguins adopt extra eggs to raise their own chicks."

"Good to know. Check out what else is in the bag, little one."

Tate wrinkles his nose as he pulls out the story book I bought for him. He lets it dangle from his fingers like a used tissue or a live scorpion, something of that ilk. "Oh. It's a book. Thank you, Daddy." He tacks on the polite words, even though I can tell he'd rather have received just about anything else. Good to know my boy isn't into the picture books. Considering how much he loved the penguin story I told him at the play party, I thought he'd be into some new penguin related material for bedtime.

"Yeah, a penguin book." I take the book from him. "And Tango Makes Three. It's about gay penguins adopting a chick."

"Oh. Cool. I guess you can read it to me later?" He perks up at the description. He must just not be a big reader. Although he seems to enjoy the bedtime stories I've read to him from my ereader during our evening phone calls.

"Sure. Not in the mood for stories right now?" I ask.

Tate shrugs, takes a deep breath like he wants to say something, then shakes his head and sighs. "Not really. Sorry, Daddy."

"It's fine. I ordered a copy of *Scamper the Penguin*. The only legit service where I could find it on streaming was region locked to the US and had no English audio. I ended up tracking down a VHS copy online. We've got an intern at the studio who is studying digital media at UBC and I guess the university media lab has a service where you can digitize old tapes. I was going to get it converted, but it hasn't arrived yet, so we'll have to watch something else in the meantime."

Tate gives me a stunned look. "You did all that for me?"

"Well, yeah? I wanted to make you smile. There's some bath stuff too, since you mentioned liking bubble baths with Daddy before bed."

"You're the best, Daddy. Thank you." He gloms onto me, wrapping his brawny arms around my neck for a smothering hug before he leans in to kiss my cheek. His enthusiastic bear hug presses us together from chest to groin. The closeness has me aching for the day when he's ready to go beyond hugs and chaste kisses, but I already agreed to slow. We are taking this at his pace, no matter how sexy he is when he lets go of his reserve. "Can we play for a bit?"

"Sure. I've got dinner in the oven, but there's time. I wasn't sure what you'd like as far as toys and stuff. If you want to order some more, we can browse toys later. Since I don't have a ton of little gear here, would you want to cuddle and have screen time? Or I can probably find something for drawing? I've got some games on my tablet from the last time I got to hang out with some littles."

"Your ex?" Tate asks warily. "Do you still want to be her daddy?"

"No. But she'll always be special to me." I answer honestly. "Is that a problem?" After being Kel's Mommy for years, I don't think I can ever turn off the part of me that cares about her. I'm not wired to stop loving someone, even if the way I love her has changed. It *has* changed, though. I love Kel as a friend now. As someone who helped me discover who I am and who I helped to grow into herself.

Tate considers for a minute, then shakes his head. "No. I don't think so? I guess I like the idea that even if we break up, you'd still be someone I could count on to care about me?"

"Always. I can't promise that we'll be perfectly compatible, but I can promise that I don't turn my back on the people I care about. And I am coming to care about you quite a lot, Tate." I pat his hand, where it's resting on the back of my couch.

Tate gives me a lopsided grin. "Cool. Tablet time now?"

"Sure, let me grab it. And then you can sit on Daddy's lap while you play. If you want."

His eyes go soft and hooded, and I can tell he's tempted by the offer. He bites his lip and watches me with an intensity that makes it clear he's worried about something he isn't saying.

"It's okay if you'd rather sit next to me." I backtrack at his hesitation, not wanting to push him too fast. "We can cuddle as much or as little as you want, okay? I don't expect anything sexual from you tonight."

Tate relaxes at the clarification. His face lights up, and I can see the transformation in him as he nods. His whole body gets in on it until he bounces on his toes and gives me a wide-eyed grin. "Yes, please, Daddy. Go get my games, please." Tate demands.

"Sure. Get comfy and I'll grab my tablet." I shoo him toward the seating area. Tate dashes around the couch. I follow him, grabbing my tablet from the side table and scrolling to find something suitable for a little. There's an alphabet game where you pop bubbles with letters in them that Kel downloaded last time I visited her. That should work. Kel got so into popping all the bubbles, it was adorable.

Tate makes grabby hands as soon as I approach, so I hand over the game. "Be careful not to drop it, precious."

"What games do you have?" he demands, all eager energy. As soon as he sees the game I've selected, his face falls. "Oh. ABCs." Tate sullenly taps at the screen, popping bubbles at random. Well, I screwed that up. The boy looks crestfallen.

"You don't like educational games?" I ask, hoping he'll volunteer the missing data I need to fix whatever upset him.

Tate shakes his head, letting the tablet rest on his lap. The game sits ignored as it encourages him to tap the letter 'B'.

"No ABC's?" I suggest.

Tate gives a tentative nod. His thumb goes to his mouth, and he sucks. The gesture revises my guess about how young he's acting down a little. No problem, I can handle whatever Tate has to throw at me.

"That's fine. Would you rather practice colors? Or just pop all the bubbles?" I take the tablet and go back to the menu screen.

"Pop 'em all," Tate slurs around his thumb. So I change the mode and hand the tablet back to him. He doesn't stop sucking his thumb, but he snuggles into my side and starts gingerly tapping the bubbles. As the first few pop, he glances toward me for encouragement.

"Wow, you're doing great. Can you pop them all?" I ask. Tate nods and starts tapping more vigorously. Soon he's got the entire screen cleared. As the last bubble pops, a celebratory fireworks animation plays and the game congratulates him on his popping skills.

"I got 'em all." Tate beams at me, thumb still caught between his lips.

"You did." I offer him a high five and he slaps my palm three times with his free hand.

"Again?" He shoves the tablet in front of me to start a new game for him.

"Sure, buddy. Want to sit on Daddy's lap while you play?" I pat my thigh and Tate glances over at me appraisingly. He nods, thumb still in his mouth.

"Yes, please."

We rearrange so that he can settle on my thighs. It takes a bit of shifting around to find a comfortable position to fit his larger frame in my lap. He has to turn sideways, his tush on one of my legs, feet propped on the couch cushion beside us, and his head nestled against my opposite shoulder.

"Comfy?" I check when he snuggles into my chest. Tate nods, head nuzzling into me with the motion.

"Play again?" He nudges the tablet toward me. I reset his game.

Tate goes back to tapping while I bask in the warm glow of holding someone close.

I savor the new twist on a familiar sensation. This is the physical affection I've missed the most since I gave up being with a little. I used to love when Kel sat with me. There is something so right about holding my little close and knowing that my presence comforts them. But despite how much I loved almost everything else about this kind of intimacy, there was always a subtle wrongness to having Kel pressed against my squishy chest. A certain dread that made my skin crawl.

That sense of disproportionate uneasiness only got worse when they pawed at my chest or nuzzled against my oversensitive nipples. At the time, I brushed it off as an aversion to nursing an adult baby. In the years since, I've learned to recognize that crawling sensation in other areas—dysphoria. That's no longer an issue. I am more than happy with the planes of my chest these days, but when Tate presses his chin against my top surgery scars, they twinge with sensation. I nudge his head higher. He sighs contentedly around his thumb as I play with his hair, unbothered by my adjusting his position.

Tate keeps playing his game. I drop my hand to his back. The fleece of his romper is soft over hard muscles. I'd happily stay like this all night.

How I've craved this cozy intimacy. The weight and heat of another person nestled into my arms. The sweet trust of a little absorbed in their interests. It's a wonderful glimpse into the future I crave with him. I indulge the urge to bury my nose in his hair and breathe in the scent of him, unfamiliar and sweet. The moment is ripe with the promise that this new start, and this precious boy, might let me truly embrace every part of myself.

CHAPTER 12

Tate

It's been ages since I got to be little in a one-on-one situation with someone new. Our community isn't huge and I'm choosy about my partners. Mostly, I don't like anyone who pressures me to be sexual in my play. That isn't what this is about for me.

Earlier, when Daddy Rory assured me, unprompted, that he wouldn't make it sexual, that was when I knew I could really do this with him. Something about him makes it easy to relax in his space.

Then he went and ruined the perfect start to the night when he offered me ABCs. I almost lost it. Like, full-on, toddler meltdown levels of losing my shit. Monty might understand my impulse to throw Daddy's tablet across the room, but I doubt anyone else would.

For a minute, I let myself indulge in visions of channeling my inner brat and watching the tablet, with its hated alphabet app, bounce across the carpeted floor. But that isn't me. Sullen withdrawal until it's over is more my speed. I've done that for my share of crappy play dates.

Daddy saves the day again, though. Not only does he notice that the game upsets me, but he changes the settings to something more fun without a fuss. He doesn't even imply that only babies don't know their letters. I do know them, but trying to decipher them is as far from fun as play can get. His calm response as he changes the settings is perfect, and he seems content to hold me while I play on the tablet.

The mindless repetition of the bubble popping game lets me sink into my little headspace. After the first game, I crawl into his lap. After a few more, the bubbles lose my interest. Monty might enjoy it. It's the sort of meditative app that he'd use to tune out the static in his overactive brain. I mostly like the fireworks at the end, and the way Daddy gives me a high five and snuggles me close when I win.

I enjoy winning. And I revel in Daddy calling me a good boy. The bubbles are boring, but Daddy's arms are warm and snuggly around me. His knee bounces me and I like that too, the gentle motion sways me against his firm chest.

"Again?" Daddy offers. I nod and then tap slowly, more focused on sucking my thumb and the drowsy warmth of being held than the game. The soft new penguin tucked in the crook of my elbow and Daddy's gentle touches lull me further. Daddy hums a song and cards his fingers in my hair. As he rocks me in his lap, I let the tablet droop against my chest.

When a buzzer sounds, I'm on the verge of dropping off for a nap. Daddy tenses under me. I glance at his face to gauge how urgent it is to move.

"Sorry, precious, but we need to get up now. Dinner's ready." Daddy pats my hip. I squirm upright as he nudges me off his lap. "We've got to get it out of the oven before it burns."

I stand, stretching tall and rubbing my eyes while I wait for Daddy to get up, too. He heads straight for the kitchen and I trail after him. "What are we having?"

"Fish sticks, french fries, and carrot sticks." Daddy lists off a few of my favorite comfort foods.

"Yummy. And ketchup?"

"Of course."

"And cookies?" I push my luck, since he got my other favorites.

"Good boys get their dessert *after* they eat their healthy food." Daddy flashes me a knowing grin over his shoulder.

"Can't we have dessert first?" I hit him with my best pleading, pouty face.

From the way he is watching me, I'm pretty sure he finds me irresistible. That heated gaze tips me out of my little headspace and more toward playing a role for daddy. Both options have their appeal, but there is a definite difference between the two. And the latter is where I feel comfortable with things getting heated.

I'm not sure if I want to go there with him tonight. I mean, I want to. But I also don't know if I'm ready to go there with him again so soon. Not when he's proven to be such a thoughtful and caring Daddy so far. I don't want to risk missing out on his tender care if we bring sex into it too soon. There are so many reasons I keep sex and kink separate with most people. I shouldn't break my own rules just because Daddy makes me want the total package.

"Nope. Nice try, precious, but it's Daddy's job to make sure you eat your healthy food first." Daddy boops me on the nose before donning the oven mitts and taking out our dinner.

The waft of heat as he opens the oven fills the room with the familiar aroma of baked fish and freezer fries. It brings me right back to having this same meal with my mom as a kid. It's not exactly fancy, but the food is pure comfort. His menu choices confirm Rory listened when I told him my preferences during our many phone calls. "Now, let's wash up for dinner."

I heave a beleaguered sigh. "Help me, Daddy?"

I offer my hands to him plaintively. He smiles as he guides me to the sink to help me lather up with foamy soap. While I scrub and hum the birthday song to myself, Daddy tests the water to be sure it isn't too hot for little hands. When he's got it just right, he stands behind me and helps me rinse away all the suds. Daddy passes me a clean towel to dry off, patting each hand for me. He makes me giggle by flapping the towel at my stomach when I give it back to him.

"Daddy! My tummy isn't wet. You don't need to dry it." I squirm away from his rogue toweling and Daddy laughs as he sets the towel aside and opens his cupboard to get us plates.

"Does my boy want a big boy plate or a kiddo plate?"

"Kiddo plate, please." I point toward the brightly colored plastic set that's stacked next to his boring adult plates.

Daddy grins and pulls out a divided plate with a cartoon penguin wearing red ear muffs. "What do you think?"

"Cute." I nod my approval. It looks brand new. Like he bought it just for me and that thought has me giddy. He planned this whole evening just for me. I bounce on my toes and kiss his cheek. "Thank you, Daddy."

Daddy cups my cheek and holds my face close to his. For a second, I think he's going to kiss my lips, but he brushes his lips over my forehead instead. "You are very welcome, Tate. It's my pleasure to take care of you. Now, do you want your fish sticks cut up or whole?"

"Whole. For dipping." I mime dipping the sticks into my ketchup. The motion requires me to step back and create some space between us. Daddy opens up the cabinet beside the dishes.

"Juice, water, or milk?"

"Water, please."

"Sippy cup?" He holds one up for me to see. "I wasn't sure just how little you get. Would you want bottles? Or diapers?"

"Sippy cup. I only drink bottles at bedtime." I haven't been brave enough to show them to him on our bedtime video chats yet. Now that he brought it up first, I will. "And I have some diapers at home, if you are into that?" I fidget at the admission even as he fills my cup with filtered water.

"I'm into you, my precious boy. Whatever you need from Daddy, I am there for."

"Yeah?"

"Yeah." He leans in close again, close enough I'm tempted to kiss him for real. He kisses my temple and turns to fix my plate. "Sit down and Daddy will get your dinner for you."

We talk about our days over dinner, and it's very date-like. With our own twist. I'm not really little while we talk, but I'm not fully big either. Daddy seems to get that. He leans in to wipe a bit of ketchup off my face when I smear it there while gesturing with a fish stick. He gets me a refill when I drain my sippy cup and keeps my puddle of ketchup topped up in the smaller compartment on my plate.

After we eat, we watch a penguin movie snuggled together on his couch. He lets me lie half on his lap, one thumb in my mouth and the other hand clutched around my new stuffie. Rory holds me, but there's nothing sexual about it, as promised. His tender caresses make me feel cherished. I don't want our evening to end when the credits roll.

"It's getting late," Rory comments when I sit up and blink drowsily at him.

"Should I head home?" I ask reluctantly. As I shift out of my little headspace, I stretch next to him. I know I should leave. We'll have time for sleepovers later.

"That might be for the best. We're taking this slow, right?" Rory rubs at his neck. He sounds like he'd rather keep me here, and that hint that he reciprocates my feelings makes excitement bubble low in my belly.

"Yeah. That's the smart move. I really like you." I lean my head into his shoulder, soaking in more of his touch before I have to leave.

"Me too. There's no rush, precious." He stands and hands me my new penguin. I hug Spot to my chest, ignoring the picture book that came with him. Daddy notices and stacks the book on top of his tablet. "I'll keep this here to read to you later. Sound good?"

"Yes. That sounds perfect, Daddy." He walks me to the door and helps me into my jacket, bending to zip it up for me. It once again covers the top of my onesie so I won't stand out on my drive home. I pause with one hand on the doorknob, not quite ready to leave him.

"Can I give you a goodnight kiss?" Daddy asks.

I nod, already leaning in with my lips puckered. Daddy meets me halfway. He cups the back of my head. It starts out sweet until I moan at the firm press of his lips on mine. Then his grip tightens. I want so much more with him.

I let my mouth soften against Rory's lips, inviting him to claim more. His tongue playing at the seam of my lips reminds me of our hookup. I open to him, half-hoping that he'll take this further than a chaste kiss and half-afraid that I'll let this go too far, too fast. That I'll fall before I can be sure he'll stick around to catch me.

Rory pulls back, leaving me breathless and aching for more of him. I stare at his mouth for a second, licking my lips to chase his taste. He smiles knowingly at me. "Patience, little one." He presses another kiss to my forehead, then steps back. "Call me when you get home and I'll read your bedtime story to you, okay?"

"Okay, Daddy." I nod obediently and leave before I do something reckless.

CHAPTER 13

Tate

Most months, I look forward to D&D with my friends. We've got a fun group. Harry might not be part of our usual kinky shenanigans, but he's really cool about it if we get to talking about our latest exploits. Cool, as in he specifically told us he's fine with us talking about our kinks around him.

This week, part of me would rather be driving to Daddy's place than going to pick up Monty to give him a ride to Harry's. I love my friends, but this thing with Rory is still new and exciting. Rory said I can come over after the game, at least. It might be hard to hide my excitement about getting to play with him again.

I know I should tell my friends about Daddy. Monty, Q, Connor and I are close. We share pretty much everything. Too much, according to several of our respective exes. But Rory is special. He ticks all my boxes so well, I'm afraid talking about him will somehow jinx this thing we're building.

When I dish with my buddies about club hookups and casual play dates, there's nothing truly private about that. Half the time, I play with the same caretakers we all know at Adventures anyway, so it's a public venue and at least one of them is also around somewhere. It's never meant something the way my time with Rory leaves me happy and fulfilled.

And it's not like I've been hiding anything. Con and Q have seen me play with Rory at several parties since that first one.

He's come with me to our last couple of munches, too. But Monty missed all those events in favor of spending time with his not-so-mysterious mystery daddy.

Monty is the only one who doesn't know about Daddy because he hasn't been around and that stings. I *know* Monty is hiding something, and I know why. He's a terrible liar and there's only one person he'd feel the need to hide that he's dating from me. I mean, unless he met someone who isn't part of the scene, but I doubt that.

I want Monty to share his happy news with me. It hurts that he hasn't yet. If he tells me about his daddy, then it might be easier to tell him about mine. Except for the first time, possibly ever, Monty doesn't take the bait to get something off his chest. He stubbornly deflects instead of telling me he's dating Luke when I give him the chance. We dance around it on the car ride to Harry's, but Monty avoids answering.

His uncharacteristic restraint is almost enough to convince me that Monty and Luke haven't said anything because there is nothing to tell. Until a latex-free condom falls out of his bag and onto our gaming table. I recognize the wrapping. It's the same brand I've seen in my brother's bathroom cabinets while hunting for a new toilet roll. It's not the fact of the object that bothers me. I couldn't care less that my best friend is carrying around my brother's preferred brand of condoms. It's the guilty look he shoots my way as he hastily covers it up and stuffs it back into the depths of his bag that seals the deal like a gut punch.

Busted. Monty has never shown a hint of guilt about his sex life around me before. That plus Luke's latex allergy and both of their general weirdness this summer and I just know that my suspicions are true.

Up to now, I've been trying to give them both space to figure out their relationship and how they want to share it with the rest of us. Monty has mooned over my brother off and on since they first met. Not pushing seemed like the best response. But now that he's all but confirmed they're an item by pointedly leaving me out of the loop, it rubs me the wrong way. I don't want their relationship to drive a wedge between me and two of the most important people in my life. It's too reminiscent of how my relationship with Gary isolated me from my closest friends. I'm not going to let that happen with Luke or Monty, they aren't going to pull away from me without a fight.

Still, our game session isn't the time or place to bring it up. I know how insecure Monty can be about relationships. And Luke has always been tight-lipped about his love life with me. Still, it might be better to reach out to Luke in private first. I don't want to force Monty into feeling like he has to tell before he's ready. And if I drop my relationship news now, he might take that as pressure to share about Luke. I don't want to pressure him. Even if he is being ridiculous to think I wouldn't want him and Luke to be happy together.

And then there's Connor to consider. If Monty and I both found a partner, that would leave Connor as the last single person in our close group of four. I don't want to rub that in his face by bringing up Rory. Not when he's been trying to date for ages and keeps striking out. I mean, I guess Harry is still single.

Technically, Daddy and I aren't exclusive yet. We talked about preferring monogamy, but sex still isn't part of what we share. Regardless, he's the only one I want to have in my bed. He's the one I imagine fucking me when I get personal with my toys recently. And he said he's content to wait for me to be ready. Even if I'm never ready. So maybe we are exclusive?

Ugh. I could just ask my friends what they think. Except I don't want to get into the nuances of my sex life with them. I want to have that discussion with Daddy. My thoughts circle the issue for most of our gaming session.

By the end of it, I'm not any closer to telling my friends what's going on with Rory and me. And I think I might have agreed to accompany Connor to a singles mixer when I was only half paying attention. Hopefully Daddy won't mind when I explain I'm going as moral support. He'd probably be happy for me to help a friend.

I don't want him to be jealous, per se. But it strikes me that if he is still casual enough about us that he expects me to be dating other people, that would hurt. I don't want to think of him with someone else. And I want him to feel the same. Which is something we ought to discuss.

The twist of hurt at the thought of Rory not caring if I'm with someone else brings me abruptly to two conclusions about our relationship. The first is that I'm ready to ask Daddy for sex. I love his tender care of me when I'm little, and I trust him enough by now to extend that to the bedroom. Besides, my heart is already fully involved in the relationship.

If I want him to be my daddy when I'm big as well as when I'm little, then sex is the next logical step. Well. Sex and other forms of intimacy. And now that I've had a few months to get to know him, I'm ready to take that step. I'm ready to mix the intense emotional with the physical and the sexual. Ready to give him and this relationship my all. Ready to stop having to pull away when our kisses turn steamy.

And if I want to take those big steps, I need to tell Rory about my dyslexia and visual processing disorder. It's not the sort of big disclosure that will really affect him, but people can be weirdly stuck up about my diagnosis. Even I can sometimes fall into those internalized insecurities about letting strangers see me struggle with reading and spelling. I don't want the way he sees me to change. I don't want him to turn out to be an asshole. But better to find out before I tell him I love him. The gaming table probably isn't the best place to realize I love Rory, but there it is.

My epiphany leaves me dazed. Lucky for me, it's a roleplay heavy session. So, I don't get my character killed with my inattention. My friends are all too excited about carousing with the goblin villagers we rescued last session to notice my distraction. So I fly under the radar while they go wild.

Harry is the only one who seems to pick up on my unusual silence. He's a good fit as the DM for our group, making sure we all have time to shine at our regular gaming sessions. He makes sure I get to make the most of the revels before the session wraps, drawing me in on the action without attracting the others' scrutiny.

"What about you, Tate?" He raises a brow at me, like he's asking if I'm okay when he asks what my character is doing while the others cavort.

I smile reassuringly and try to get in on the fun, and it doesn't take long for pretending to get into the game to lead to actually getting into it. The rest of the session keeps my mind off my personal life. I stop questioning how far to push Monty and Luke about their relationship, and worrying about how Daddy will react to what I want to say to him after our date tonight. For a few hours, I just get to be the brave knight errant fighting alongside my party of adventurers to save the day. I can just play a game with my closest friends while we devour our favorite snacks.

CHAPTER 14

Rory

Our first playdate at my place seals the deal for me. Tate is the boy I want to share my life with, if he'll have me. His desire to take things slow has only made it easier to fall for my sweet boy.

It creates space for us to get to know each other outside of the bedroom and I'm falling for him. But there are things I need to tell him before we get serious. Well, *more* serious than planning out weekly playdates, being a daily part of his bedtime routine and getting the privilege of him calling me daddy.

Between our busy work schedules, it's hard to arrange playdates, but we've managed to get together in person just about once a week for most of the summer. I've taken him out for impromptu lunch dates when our break times made it work. The boy needs someone to remind him he needs more than one meal a day.

More than once, when he calls to vent about an after hours emergency call out, I've been tempted to invite him to spend the night after he finishes. If nothing else, just so I can make sure he takes care of himself. At the very least, I want to pack him a proper lunch and send him off to work with his morning coffee and a full belly, but much as that feels like my job as his daddy, we aren't there yet.

I want to get there with him, though. To a place where he comes home to me after a long day so that he can let his hair down and be little. I want to have him snuggled in my arms while I read his bedtime stories to him. Be the one to fix his bedtime bottle, put on his diaper, and tuck him under the covers. I've fantasized about holding him in my arms as he drifts away to dreamland.

Not to mention all the less PG activities we could get up to in person. I want to get intimate with him again. Sexually and not. Our semi-anonymous hookup the night we met was hot, but I want to earn his trust more than I want sex.

We can pursue intimacy in other ways until he's ready for more with me. Bath time springs to mind. And getting to take care of him when he's little. From giving him a bottle to changing his diapers to having his art on my fridge. I want it all.

The last few times he came over to play, we did a bit of toy shopping. I've collected a few more toys since, so we don't have to rely on screen time now that he's picked out his favorite activities. It's fun to take him shopping. I want him to have everything he likes when he comes to my place.

He's adorable when he's little and I want him to have all the things he needs to go deep into that headspace when he plays. Spending hours building a block city around his racetrack last weekend was the most fun I've had in ages. I can't get enough of my precious boy.

Tate was so into his construction that he lost himself in the activity for hours. He ended up taking a nap on the rug with his tush in the air. I couldn't help imaging how cute he'd be with his adorable bum padded in a diaper. That's something we are saving for when he knows me better, though. More of the intimacy that we're taking slowly.

For now, it's enough that he feels comfortable being little in my space. And I like all the reminders of my boy that now clutter up my once tidy living room. I've got a box of plastic caltrops, also known as blocks, a racetrack with several brightly colored cars, and assorted other toys in bins beside my bookshelf.

He picked out two dolls for us to play with, usually alongside his penguins, and some coloring books, too. I wondered how he would react when I took him into the pink shelves of the 'girl toy' area. I figured it was a good tentative step toward gauging his attitudes about gender.

To my relief, Tate didn't bat an eye about picking out a couple of dolls and some outfits to add to his toy collection. Playing with Kel and her friends, I've been around littles who turn up their noses at toys they don't think match what their gender dictates they *should* play with. It's a relief that Tate isn't one of them.

I don't care what toys he enjoys. If he likes dolls and tea parties or dinos and trucks, it's all the same to me. I'm just as happy to play house with my boy as I am to help his dinosaur figurines chase the Barbies around his racetrack. The point is that he never acts like dolls are beneath him or as if his gender is a strict set of rules to be adhered to at all times.

I mean, the fact he has close friends who are trans and never seems to slip up on their pronouns made me trust that I'm safe with him since our first munch together. His easy acceptance of his friends gives me confidence that he'll respond well to my gender history. Still, there is a vast difference between caring about a trans friend and being in love with a trans partner. So I know I need to tell Tate about my history soon instead of springing it on him once we've both gotten attached. Er, more attached.

I'm planning on telling Tate soon. He's come over a few times already, but this is the first time he is planning to spend the night. He comes to my place with an overnight bag after a Saturday game day with his friends, buzzing with excitement about his character and the campaign they're playing.

Tate called to tell me he was on his way after he gave Monty a ride home, so I have mac and cheese almost finished when he arrives. Not the healthiest, but I'm following my dad's recipe for adding in tuna, grated cheese and peas to at least hit multiple food groups.

We exchange greetings before Tate launches into a play-by-play of his game while busily rearranging the colorful magnetic tiles on my fridge into a tower. I mix up the sauce as I listen attentively to my boy. His face is so animated when he's excited, his enthusiasm draws me into his story. Tate pulls a yuck face when I pour the peas into the pan, interrupting the flow of his retelling. I level him with a stern look and an admonishment to try new foods, and he agrees to give peas a chance.

He smooshes his tower flat against the fridge, scattering several magnetic tiles across the floor. He glances my way, as if to check if he's in trouble. "Oops, sorry, Daddy."

"Pick those up, please." I remind him. So he does, sticking them back to the fridge in a series of clacks.

He rearranged the tiles into a colorful pattern framing one of his pictures, then plops himself down at the table to wait. Tate fiddles with the kid friendly utensils I laid out for him to use while I finish stirring and plating our food. I let his words wash over me, enjoying his excitement. He's in an in-between space right now. He's not little, but he's got that little energy where he bounces with excitement as he talks a mile a minute about his interests. Tate swings his feet idly under the table, no mean feat with his long legs.

"So, we were the guests of honor at a big feast, because we rescued a bunch of hostage villagers for the goblin king. It was all fun and games until Harry ended the session on a cliffhanger with the big bad taking over the goblin king to give us a message. Like, mind meld or something. But before we leave on our next quest, my kobold knight is getting a new set of enchanted armor. Harry let me haggle for a huge discount since we rescued the armorer's wife and their kid. It's going to be epic."

"Yeah? What does your new armor do?" I ask as I pour us both some water, his in a sippy cup. "Wash up before you eat, please."

"Yep." He stands to wash his hands. "It gives me magical resistance. Which is good, because the big baddy paladin has a wizard and a sorcerer under his command. So they've got some nasty spells that almost got us all killed last time we faced them." Tate pauses for breath. I slide his cup and his penguin bowl in front of his place setting. "Thank you, Daddy." Tate beams at me and it takes all my willpower to resist the urge to pull him into my lap and kiss him silly. But mac and cheese doesn't reheat well and we aren't having sex tonight. Regardless of how much I want him. Far better not to tempt myself with thoughts of doing things that aren't happening yet.

"Dig in, Tater-Tot." I gesture to his plate, then take my first bite as I watch him pick through his food to avoid getting any peas on his fork. His face lights up in a big grin as he chews his first bite. "Is it good?"

Tate nods vigorously. "Yep, super yummy. Daddy makes the cheesiest KD ever." He underscores that assertion by scooping up a much more generous forkful and zooming it toward his mouth like an airplane.

"KD?" I ask.

"Kraft Dinner?" he says, like it's the most obvious thing ever. "This." He points at his plate.

"Ah, I was wondering about the label on the box. Is that a Canadian thing?" I take a sip of my water. Most things here are pretty similar to when I lived south of the border, but that almost makes the differences more jarring. Like how my car insurance is basically the equivalent of my registration down south and the BC provincial plan is the only auto insurer around.

Tate shrugs. "Guess it is. That's what we've always called it."

"Weird. And my boy likes his KD?"

"Yep. I like it extra cheesy. And it's not too bad with the peas."

"Good. You don't eat enough veggies."

Tate sticks his tongue out at me. He turns the rude gesture into licking his fork when I narrow my eyes at him. He gives me a big wide-eyed innocent look and I can't help laughing.

"What?" Tate asks.

"Nothing. Eat your dinner and then we can play for a while before bath time."

CHAPTER 15

Tate

I'm not sure how long I've been playing with my blocks when Daddy nudges my shoulder. Just that time has passed, and the sun is down. I cover my yawn with my fist and Daddy smiles at me.

"It's getting late, huh? You still want to stay the night?" he asks. "Just to sleep, I mean. I want to put you to bed in person."

"Yes, please. I told you I wanted that, too." I smile at him. He hasn't been pushy up to now, so I trust him not to ask for more than I'm ready for tonight. And cuddling with my daddy all night long sounds too good to pass up the chance. We don't get to see each other in person nearly enough.

Business has been booming all spring and summer. Between old clients and new construction, I've got contracts for days. Today has been a well-earned and much needed break from my adult responsibilities. I'm not ready for the day to be over yet. Rory reaches out to comb his fingers through my hair.

"Good. So. Bath time?" Daddy rubs his hands together briskly. Like it's an effort not to touch me more. I want him to touch me, but I'm still not quite ready to jump into anything sexual with my daddy. With Rory, sure. But with my daddy? We aren't there yet and I don't trust myself to keep the two categories separate. He points toward his washroom.

"You want to see me naked, Daddy?" I tease him before I can think through my words.

"Always. But only if you're good with that?"

"Totally." I might not be ready for sex, but bath time doesn't have to be sexual. It can just be my daddy taking care of me. Tender and intimate.

Daddy runs the bathwater, pouring in a generous amount of lavender scented bubbles. "I got these color tablets, too. Did you want to pick one?"

"Blue." I reach for the tablet and drop it into the water, watching the colors swirl as the tub fills with water and a growing mass of bubbles. The washroom is cozy, warm and steamy with the door closed when Daddy turns off the water.

"Let's get you out of your clothes now, precious."

I lift my arms and let him do most of the work of stripping me. Daddy eases my arms out of the sleeves of my soft t-shirt. He tickles my belly as soon as it's bared, then gently unbuttons my pants and slides them partway down my legs.

He pauses when he reveals the superhero undies I have on under the outfit and gives me a lopsided grin. "Is my boy a hero?"

"Yep. A superhero." I puff out my chest to show him my best hero pose.

"Very nice." He nods solemnly. "What's your superpower?"

"I'm super speedy. Want to see?"

"Not on the slippery tiles. Maybe you can show me how super fast you are when you get dressed after tubby time?"

"Okay." I nod. "The tub is slippery when it's wet."

"Yes, it is, and Daddy needs his boy to be safe around water."

"Uh, huh. Can I get in now?"

Daddy checks the water with his fingers and nods. "Yep, it's perfect. Hop right in."

I take that literally, hopping up to the edge of the tub. "Watch your step." Daddy takes my elbow to steady me. Right, slippery. We talked about that, so I let Daddy help me into the nice deep water.

The bath is perfectly warm as it laps against my belly. It's fun to have the bubbles cover my legs and come up to my tummy in his oversized tub. The deep water reminds me of bath time as a kid. When it felt like I could float in the tub and splash away all my cares along with the dirt from a long day of playing outside.

"Want to wash yourself or let Daddy take care of you?" Daddy holds up an owl shaped terry cloth glove.

"You can do it, please." I smile at him. First, Daddy washes my hair. He massages the shampoo into my scalp, then carefully has me lie back so he can rinse it out to avoid getting any suds in my eyes. Next, Daddy uses the glove to wash me. His touch all over my body makes me feel cared for and connected to him in a way that sex can't come close to beating.

His gentle touch borders on reverent as he washes my groin and I watch his face as he takes care of me. He wants me, but he doesn't make that my problem or linger there. This is why I love having a daddy. It's a different way of being intimate and showing love. A softer place where I can be vulnerable with a partner in ways that I can't as the big burly man I am in my workaday life.

Daddy moves on to my legs, and I giggle and squirm, holding in my hilarity as he rubs the cloth under my knees. I can't help myself when he gets to my feet, though. My legs flail, splashing bubbles all over him as he grips the arches of my feet.

"Does that tickle, precious?" Daddy teases as I giggle uncontrollably and pull my foot free from his grasp.

"Yes! Again." I shove my foot toward him when I've got my giggles under control.

"Daddy's little boy likes tickles?" He crooks his fingers at me, like he's getting ready to launch a full scale tickle attack.

"Uh huh," I giggle in expectation. Daddy wiggles his fingers at me and I clench up in a little ball to protect my underarms and neck from being a tempting target.

"Hm. Not in the tub. Can you wash your own toes or do you think I can do it if I use more pressure?"

"I can hold still." I offer him my foot again. Daddy wipes the soapy cloth between my toes quickly. I still wriggle and have to bite my lip against laughing at the squirmy feeling of having someone else touch me there.

"And the other one?" He sets down my right foot and I offer him my left.

I like how he asked about tickles. When I'm little, I love being tickled. But only when I trust the person doing it to stop if I need them to. I trust Daddy. That might seem fast to some people, after only a handful of playdates, but I feel like I know him well already.

This is the man who has been exchanging silly GIFs of his day with me. He makes time to call to put me to bed every night for the past couple of months. He listens to me and doesn't push my limits. At least not in a bad way. He wouldn't abuse my trust. I know what that looks like and it isn't this.

"There, all clean." Daddy presses a kiss to the top of my foot, then releases it. "Want to play for a bit?"

"Yes!"

"I got you some bath toys. Want to see?"

"Yes, please." I make grabby hands and Daddy chuckles at my eagerness.

"Let me get them." Daddy ruffles my hair, then reaches for the bag that held the bubble bath and color tablets. He pulls out two little plastic boats and two penguin figurines that he removes the tags from before handing them to me. There is something else in the bag, but he makes no move to remove it.

"Is there something else in there?" I ask, curiosity getting the better of me.

"Just these." He pulls out a package of foam letters. "I got them when we first discussed playtime. Now that I know you better, I'm thinking you don't want these, do you?"

"No." I agree, pleased that he isn't pushing them on me. I can tell he's curious, and probably putting pieces together about my avoidance of lengthy texts. The big part of me knows I need to tell him what I have against alphabet toys and games soon, but for now I can just be little with him.

"No problem." Daddy tucks the bag closed and sets it aside. He sits, content to watch me play with the little penguins and their boats. I get him to do the voices of the sentient ships for me as I splash around until my fingers are all wrinkly and the water cools.

"All done." I stand up, shivering in the cooler air.

"Let's get you ready for bed." Daddy wraps me in a warm towel, pats me dry and helps me brush my teeth before he leads me to his room.

Rory's got more new presents laid out on his bed. A pajama with polar bears and penguins eating ice cream on it and another story book. "You get in your jammies and I'll grab your penguins. Did you need anything else? What would you like to drink in your bedtime bottle?" He has seen me with them on our video chats, but this is the first time he's fixing it for me. That drives home the fact that we're really doing this sleepover thing.

"Water." I grab his hand before he can leave and pull him close to kiss his cheek. "Thank you, Daddy."

"It's my pleasure, precious." He strokes my cheek with our faces inches apart and I want him to kiss me. Really kiss me, but he steps away to let me change into my warm new pajamas in privacy. "Get cozy in bed for your bedtime story, okay?"

"Okay, Daddy." I don't want him to leave, but it's probably for the best not to rush things. But as he turns to go, I'm disappointed about it. I put my bag in here earlier and I hesitate over whether to grab the diapers from there or put on the undies he laid out with my new pajamas. If I'm wearing a diaper with him, I want Daddy to be the one to put it on me. "Wait!" I call for him as he steps into the hall. Daddy turns and gives me a questioning glance.

"Help me get dressed?"

"Of course." He smiles at me. "I wasn't sure how much help you'd want, but I love helping my boy."

"Diaper?" I ask, pointing at my overnight bag. I tense, waiting for the response. We've talked about diapers before. He knows I wear them sometimes and I know he is fine with changing me, in theory. It's still a big step to take, at least in my head. I'm trusting him to take care of my most basic physical needs, and that comes with a lot of emotions.

Daddy grabs my bag, pulls out the cute custom penguin reusable diaper and smiles at me. "This is going to be so cute on your little tush. Are you ready for a change, precious?"

I nod and perch on the edge of his bed. Daddy comes over. He sets down my bag. Our gazes meet and his eyes are so full of love that it doesn't leave me any room to second guess taking this step with him. I am falling for Rory. There's no doubt left in my mind about it.

Daddy tips me onto my back on the mattress, supporting my head as I recline. I let him maneuver me into position, my brain flashing unhelpfully to when he put me on my back to fuck me the night we met. That was a damn good night, and maybe we'll have more like it soon, but not tonight. Tonight is about a deeper connection than just bodies and sex.

Daddy ignores my growing erection as he lifts my legs up to situate the diaper under me. He tucks my half-hard bits into the soft fabric, folds the diaper into place with the ease of someone who has done this before. He fastens the snaps so that it fits snug around my body.

"There, nice and cozy and ready for bedtime." Daddy blows a raspberry on my tummy. I giggle and curl away from him, pushing his head away. Daddy captures my hands. "That's right, you're ticklish, huh?"

"Yeah."

"Want Daddy to stop?"

I nod. "Want kisses."

So Daddy leans over my body to give me what I want. He braces his hands on either side of my shoulders as he smacks loud kisses all over my face until I squirm and gasp his name in protest. "Daddy! Not there."

"Where then?" He asks, pretending to be confused. "On your toes?"

"Here," I point to my lips and Daddy gives me a gentle kiss on the mouth before standing upright. I miss the heat of his body and the sense of being boxed in by him. My diaper is getting tighter as my erection grows. It's probably just as well that he pulls back when he does, even if part of me wouldn't mind going much further than kissing.

"Do you need help with your jammies?"

"I can do it myself." Might make it easier to keep our hands, and other parts, to ourselves that way.

"Okay, then I'll go get that bottle for you while you get dressed."

I watch him leave before I stir myself to pull on the soft new pajamas. They're a perfect fit and the cotton is soft against my skin. I take a minute to admire all the different ice cream flavors the pajama penguins are eating before I crawl into bed.

Daddy returns with his arms full of Fuzzy and Spot, who I left sitting in their block castle. He's also got the penguin book he bought me for our first date at his place tucked under one arm and a bottle in his other hand. I take my penguin stuffies and the bottle.

Daddy settles on the edge of his bed and I snuggle close to him to listen to my story. I focus on the pictures as he reads, then cuddle up to him when he sets the book aside to join me under the covers. I wriggle until I've got my diapered butt pressed against Daddy's body. He kisses my neck and holds me tight in response. His arms around me and the steady rhythm of his breathing lull me to sleep.

CHAPTER 16

Rory

Tate, fast asleep in my arms first thing in the morning, is pure bliss. He rotated in his sleep, so that he's facing me and his peaceful expression melts my heart. My boy is sprawled half on top of my chest, arms wrapped around me and his two stuffies. Is it any wonder I can't muster the motivation to bother him by getting out of bed?

Instead of disturbing his slumber, I hold him tighter and kiss the crown of his head. He still seems to be asleep, so I hold him while I try to memorize the feel of a warm sleep-pliant boy in my arms. I run my hands along his back, the cotton of his pajamas soft under my fingers. Tate sighs and snuggles his face into my chest.

"Five more minutes," he mumbles, still more than half asleep.

I stifle a laugh. "You can sleep in as long as you want, precious." Getting an actual response seems to rouse him to true wakefulness.

He lifts his head and meets my gaze with a smile. "Hm, you're a good pillow." He rests his cheek back on my chest, his warm breath ghosts over my nipple through the thin fabric of my undershirt. It tickles a little, and I try to ignore thoughts of his hot mouth on me there. It's not something I've ever let myself enjoy. Too much dysphoria around my chest when I was with Kel and I haven't had a regular partner since I got top surgery. Someone I can be tender with instead of intimacy focusing on getting each other off as the only goal.

With Tate, touching is a reward unto itself. I love holding him while he dozes. Or sitting next to him when he watches a cartoon. Washing him and helping with his diaper last night was pure perfection. The trust in his eyes as I doted on him is intoxicating. I could get off on his wordless obedience as I asked him to give me access to every part of him, from his hair down to his ticklish toes. He didn't question whether I'd take pains not to get stinging soap in his eyes, just accepted that I would take care of him. All of him is a delight.

My libido is very interested in those memories. But, it's just as well I don't get hard without a little help from the pump in my balls. I don't want a raging erection to curtail these sweet morning snuggles. And no sooner do I have that thought than Tate shifts to rub his erection against my thigh.

The thick padding of his diaper makes me second guess whether that's really what I'm feeling, at first. Tate grinds against me, almost subconsciously seeking his pleasure. I rest one hand on his diapered ass, resisting the urge to encourage him. His sexy wiggling is hot as hell, but he said he isn't ready to include sex in our play. So I'll respect his boundaries, no matter how much I'd love to hold him close and rut our dicks together.

I pause in rubbing his back with my other hand. "Is my precious boy hard?"

"Yeah." Tate freezes, dick pressing into my thigh, a tantalizing promise of where this morning could lead. "Sorry." He squirms off of me and rolls to sit next to me instead. "You make me want things."

"Things?" I sit up too, not turning to face him, since sometimes it's easier to talk without having to meet anyone's gaze. I offer him my hand, and he takes it, squeezing hard. He doesn't turn toward me either.

"Sexy things. Things I rarely do with the bigs I play with." Tate blows out his breath in a noisy gust.

"Is there a reason for that?" I squeeze his fingers. Tate rubs his thumb over my knuckles.

"Yeah." Tate draws in a deep breath, holds it for a second and then he explains. "I get too attached. I want it to mean something."

"Did our hook up mean something?"

"No." Tate drops his head onto my shoulder. "That's different." He straightens back up and lifts one hand. "Meaningless sex is fine." He raises the other hand. "And casual playtime, as a little, is fine. But put them together and…it all goes to pieces." Tate clasps his hands together, then flings them apart. His mouth forms an explosion sound effect that makes me want to tug him into my lap and tell him how adorable he is. But that wouldn't be giving his words the weight they deserve, so I refrain.

"What goes to pieces?" I ask.

"My stupid heart, usually." His dry huff of a laugh sounds more pained than amused. "I fall fast when sex is vulnerable in the way it gets when I'm with my daddy. If a vanilla guy took the time to be sweet with me around sex, it might be the same. I don't know. Something about the guy who is fucking me, also taking care of me, seeing my squishy emotional bits…It just makes it hard to turn that off. The caring. Heck, even if I'm the one taking care of my partner, it gives me all these tender feelings that are hard to shake."

Tate turns to peek at me, and I nod my understanding. "It's too intimate to share with just anyone, right?" I suggest.

"Yeah. That's it. Pretty much. So, I stopped sharing it." He shrugs. "What we've got is too good to rush. But I get it if you're sick of waiting around until I'm ready."

"I'll wait as long as you need. You know I enjoy sex, but I don't need it to be happy with you." I still want him as much now as I did that first night. More even. But that's only a fraction of what I want with him.

"I believe you, but I want to be ready. Soon."

"No rush." I put my arm around his shoulders and pull him back into my side. He melts into my embrace, resting his head on my shoulder again. I kiss the top of his head and wrap my other arm around him too, holding my boy close. He's being so open with me; I need to return that trust. "There's something I've been meaning to tell you. Before we get any more serious."

"You've got a deep, dark secret?" Tate teases, nudging my ribs with his elbow until I ease up on the hug.

"That might be overstating it." I jostle him gently from side to side before letting him go.

"That's cool. I've got some stuff I should probably share with you, too. Nothing that will affect you much, but things you should know about me, if we're getting serious." Tate hugs me tight around my middle.

"You can tell me anything." I pat his head where he's got it burrowed into my gut.

"Yeah, I think I can. You can go first, though. What's your thing?" Tate tips his head back to glance up at me without pulling out of our embrace.

"It's nothing major. Like you said, nothing that would impact you much, but I was AFAB." I explain, pretty sure he's had enough exposure to trans people to know the abbreviation for assigned female at birth.

"Yeah." Tate nods. "I'd guessed as much."

"You did?" I brace for whatever he might say next, knowing it might suck to hear all the ways he might have clocked that I'm trans.

"Yeah. You have that pronoun pin with the trans flag on it. I saw it on your shirt that first night. Not that cis guys can't share their pronouns, but the flag makes it seem like you're part of the community. That, plus the scars...I figured you might be trans. It doesn't change anything between us." Tate furrows his brow in thought. "Is your transition why you stepped away from being a daddy for a while?"

"Yes," I admit. "It seems silly now, but it was hard for me to get my head around going from being Kel's Mommy to being a daddy. Or even just a caregiver. I had a lot of internalized misogyny and transphobia to work through to realize that my need to nurture and take care of a little isn't gendered. It's just part of who I am without defining anything else about me."

Tate hugs me tighter. "I'm glad you worked through your issues, because so far, you're the perfect daddy for me."

I smile at his high praise. "Thank you, Tate. That's fitting, since you're the perfect boy for me. Did you have questions about my transition or anything?"

"Not really? I mean. If there is anything you want to talk about, I'm all ears. Or if you need to vent about the pharmacy being out of T. Or if you have a day where dysphoria gets you down, I want to be there for you. But you don't owe me all your personal medical information. I mean, I know your dick works. Like, really fucking well." He gives me a cheeky wink and the hand he has resting near my hip drifts toward my groin.

I chuckle, but swat his hand away from my junk so we can talk. "It works better than I'd have dared to hope when I was saving every penny for the medical expenses and gritting my teeth through painful electrolysis appointments."

"Hm, well, I think I'd like to take it for another ride soon." His hand drifts along my thighs. I gently place it closer to my knee. "I'm thinking you don't share that information with just anyone?" Tate asks on a more serious note.

"You're going to kill Daddy if you keep teasing me." I pat his hand to encourage him not to move it. He takes the hint and stops with the roving hands. "You may have noticed that I'm not exactly stealth. I mean, you saw my pin. I wear it most of the time. And I have an IMDB profile with roles from pre-transition, so the dots are there for people to connect. Not that I'm a big enough celebrity for the public at large to care. I got them to switch over my name and include my roles from when I presented as a woman early in my career, so the information is out there. But yeah, I told you because I trust you. I want you to know all of me, and that's a big part of what shaped who I am."

"Awesome. So, that plays into what I wanted to tell you. I want you to know all of me, too. I know you've noticed I'm cagey around alphabet games when I'm little, and I try to avoid texting most of the time. It's because I'm dyslexic."

"Oh. So, does that mean you struggle to read?"

"Basically? Technically, I've got a visual processing disorder on top of the dyslexia, but they never really differentiated that from the dyslexia when I was a kid. So letters have always been a jumbled mess for me. No amount of hard work is going to change how my brain is wired. I *can* read if I have to, but it's difficult as heck for me and it gives me a headache to focus on most text for too long. And my spelling and handwriting suck. Some fonts are easier than others, but it's still not fun."

"I bet. Sorry I pushed the letter game on you at our play date, precious. I wish I'd known."

"You didn't push. Not like other people I've played with, anyway. You dropped it as soon as you realized it was bothering me without making a big deal or tying it to how far I'd regressed. Like sure, babies can't read, but not being able to read doesn't make me a baby. And you never insisted on me texting you back after I told you I preferred to call for anything that requires more than a few words to answer. That's something I appreciate about you. And don't worry about sending texts now that you know, I have my phone read them to me. If I need to talk more in depth, I'll ask to call, same as we've been doing. I've pretty much set up my life to accommodate my needs as much as possible. It's why Luke and I work so well as business partners. He manages all the paperwork and I handle the actual plumbing."

"Ah, so that's why you use the virtual assistant on your phone too, huh? And dictate your notes at the end of each call. I'd wondered, since it seems like extra work for both of you."

"Yep. I send Luke sound clips of what he needs to bill. He transcribes the audio for our invoicing software. During business hours, he updates anything that comes up while I'm on site and sends it to the printer I keep in my work van. For emergency calls, we send the invoice the next morning. Anyway, I'm sure there are other options out there, but our system works for us. Plus, I enjoy working with my brother."

"It's great that you two are so close. I don't keep in touch with my sister as much as I should."

"Eh, family gets complicated. Is there a reason you don't talk?"

"Mostly that we're both busy and have little in common. She's got three kids and still lives in the same neighborhood where we grew up. Whereas I have no interest in parenting an actual child and haven't lived in the same place for more than a few years since I left home for university." I shrug and change the subject since my family isn't my favorite topic. We aren't close and I've accepted that fact. "So, is the reading thing why the picture books weren't your favorite gifts when I got them for you?"

"Basically." He shrugs and picks at the blankets. "I enjoy it when you read to me. But I've had way too many partners and caretakers who thought they could magically fix me. If only I'd just try some trick that worked for someone they know, or submit to their particular brand of discipline or whatever.

Like, my mom didn't take me to every specialist in town and put me through years of one-on-one tutors touting the latest guaranteed cures." Tate rolls his eyes. "Mom even took me to a fancy optometrist for the world's worst glasses with weird tinted lenses that the other kids had an absolute field day mocking me over. Nothing really helped."

"I don't think you need to be fixed." I give him another gentle squeeze and he bounces our joined hands against the pillows.

"Right? Mom definitely meant well. She never wanted me to struggle the way she did as a single parent, trying to support me and get her education. And I mean, sure, some things would be easier if I could just get the letters and my brain to cooperate. But it's not worth the literal headache when there are workarounds that let me do what I need to do. Especially since I knew early on that I wanted to work with my hands. When I told her I had an apprenticeship lined up to become a plumber like Uncle Frank instead of going to university like Luke, we fought. I could have appeased her with trade school, but I learn better from hands-on experience."

"You mentioned taking over the business from your uncle. I assume he supported your career choices?"

"Yep, I know I strained his patience to the max when I was learning the ropes. Reading fine print instructions or contracts is still a nightmare, but I get by professionally. For everything else, my phone does a good job with the virtual assistant and I can scan important documents for my text-to-speak to read them to me. It would be great if more places had universal signage." Tate shrugs. "Like a picture of a toilet by the toilets instead of trying to get cutesy with the names, but I manage just fine."

"Totally different reasoning, but I am right there with you on that one." I nod.

"Right? How hard is it to just stick a picture of a toilet on the washroom and leave it at that?" He smiles ruefully.

"Yep, no need to make it complicated. I've seen them using more of the universal symbols on signs at places like hospitals. Like a picture of an X-ray for the radiation department, or a nurse at a desk for nurse's stations. They still have the words, but the pictures made it simpler to find my way around the hospital when I went in for my most recent surgery. Every bit helps when you're loopy on nerves, in pain, and coming down from anesthesia." I shift closer to him and he mirrors the movement. Tate once again rests his head on my shoulder and lets me wrap an arm around his back to hold him close.

"Okay, I know I said I wouldn't pry, but when you say 'most recent', it makes me wonder. How many did you have?"

"Surgeries? Several." I chuckle and pat his arm. "Don't worry about asking. I don't mind telling *you* anything you want to know about me. Getting to know each other is part of the point of dating. As for the surgeries, it started with one for my chest. My hysterectomy was a little over a year after that. Once I convinced my doctor I was positive I'd never change my mind about using it. And then four stages for my phallo, spread over about a year. I might have to get another revision to replace the erectile device at some point, just from regular wear, but that's probably another eight or more years down the road."

"That's a lot to go through. And you did it all in the US?"

"Yep." I nod.

"So, wait. Does that mean you had to pay out of pocket?" Tate lifts his head from my shoulder to look at my face again, his expression horrified. His nose wrinkles as he considers the cost.

"Ha! Nope. No way I could have afforded everything out of pocket. I just had killer insurance from my day job, including short-term disability for my post-op recovery. Only had to pay what my insurance didn't cover. Co-pays, electrolysis, travel expenses, and loads of other stuff that all added up to a lot. Took a ton of scrimping and saving and a move to Cali where the doctor I wanted to use is based. No huge hardship there, since there was more industry work to further my career around LA. And I had to go with the surgeons covered in-network.

"It all worked out that the day job covered my medical needs and the move helped me to build my demo reel and get established in the industry. Totally worth it. Even if I did up and move here right after I finished paying down the line of credit I used for the parts that weren't covered. You know, a place where it would have all been paid for under the provincial medical plan, anyway. But I can't complain. I just feel lucky that I could transition the way I needed and wanted to, you know?"

"I'm happy you got the care you needed, Daddy." Tate snuggles closer to me.

"Thank you, precious. I'm glad too."

Tate turns his face toward me, kissing my neck. His lips send jolts of pleasure straight to my groin and I groan, then push him off me. "It's not nice to tease Daddy, Tate."

Tate palms himself. "Is it sending mixed messages if I say I might want to fool around with you?"

"Just a bit." I hold up two fingers to show a small amount. "And might isn't exactly enthusiastic consent."

He sighs. "I'm sorry."

"Don't be. I meant it when I said no pressure. We can do something else."

"Or talk about sex? I feel really close to you right now. And I'd like to express that with sex. If you want? My point in holding off was not to get too attached. Turns out this whole emotional intimacy thing that we're doing here is just as hazardous for my heart as fucking you." He gestures between us and his elbow bumps me again, emphasizing just how close we're sitting. Our thighs press together more firmly as he shifts his weight.

"Are you sure?" I want to say yes to sex with him, but I want this thing to last more than I want to fuck him again.

"Yeah." Tate's reply is a breathy rasp.

I tip his chin up for a chaste kiss. "I'm falling for you, too. If that's what you're not quite saying."

"That's what I meant. And I want you to make love to me."

Part of me wants to hold off on making that call when I'm all tangled up with him in bed. But Tate is more than capable of making his own choices. He knows his limits. He was the one who wanted to go slow. If he says he's ready, then I need to trust him. And I want this. Want him. Well, he asked, and I'm not in the habit of lying to my partners. "I'd like that, too."

Tate pulls me into another kiss. This one with open mouths and tongues moving together. He kisses like he wants me to take everything I want from him. His lips mold to mine and he follows my lead. He shifts onto my lap, straddling me. His arms loop around so that he can cling to the back of my neck.

The way he holds on tight reminds me of the way he hugs me with his entire body when he's being little. There is nothing small about the way he grinds his hard erection against my dick. I reach between us to adjust myself and pump up my cock.

"Can I suck you?" Tate asks, all breathy and sweet.

"Yeah. I'm not about to say no to a blow job."

"Awesome. Anything I should know about your junk so I don't make you uncomfortable?"

"It's pretty much the same as cis junk at this point, other than needing an erectile device and staying hard until I manually deflate it. Which means I *could* fuck you all night long, but it might chafe at some point, and I usually need a break after a couple of orgasms."

"A couple, huh?"

"Yeah. I like to keep going after the first, but it gets over-sensitive if I push past the second one. Oh, and I guess my jizz dribbles more than it shoots? But like, I do ejaculate a small amount. Not everyone can, post-phallo; I lucked out with my results. So, we should probably use condoms for anything penetrative."

"Huh. That's fun, about multiple orgasms. Not a huge fan of condoms for oral."

"I get that. There's still a risk, though. Have you gotten tested recently?"

"Yep. I go twice a year, usually. My last test panel came back all negative six months ago. I'm not big on casual sex, so there's only been you since we hooked up."

"Awesome. And same. I got tested when I went in for my physical to get my work visa papers done. Figured I'd make the most of my insurance before I moved up here, since it takes three months of residency before the province will cover me."

"It does? Shoot, what if you get sick or injured before then?" Tate sounds indignant on my behalf. It's weird to realize he's so used to not worrying about medical coverage that finding out I might not have any is an affront. Another of those moments where I notice the differences between my new home and my old one.

I shrug. "I'd have had to pay out of pocket."

"That sucks." He pauses a moment, brow scrunched in concentration like he's calculating, "Oh. Has it really been three months already?"

"Four since I moved here, but who's counting? I could have

paid to keep my US plan active, but without the employer contribution it cost too much, so I figured I'd roll the dice."

"That sucks. I can't believe we've been together for months already."

"Guess you make the time fly." I tease him.

"Yeah? I want to make you fly. So, can we ditch the condoms for oral, or would you rather wait?"

"We can ditch them, since we've both gotten tested. I'd like to hold off on going bare for anal, though." I squeeze his ass through the thick cloth covering it and he grinds against me again.

"We can wait. Something to look forward to." Tate licks his lips. "I'm due for my next test soon anyway, so maybe after that?"

"That sounds perfect to me. Even if we are adding sex to this, there's still no rush."

"So long as you don't want to save it for marriage, I'm okay with not rushing," Tate quips.

"Are you proposing?" I tease him.

Tate flushes. "That's not what I meant! It's way too soon for even thinking about that."

"But is it something you want someday?"

"Not really. Gary and I were this close to going there and I can't imagine that would have ended well. Made me wary of tying my finances to someone else. But there are always prenups, so it's not a deal breaker, if you're serious about wanting that someday."

"Good to know. I don't need a piece of paper to tell the world we belong together, precious. Now, you mentioned blowing me?" I change the subject, because now that we've discussed it, I don't see any reason to hold back any longer.

"I did." Tate licks his lips and grinds into me teasingly. I groan at the sensation. The two of us rut together until Tate gets frustrated with all the layers between us blunting the friction. He slithers off my lap to pull my cock free from my boxers.

He licks a broad stripe over the head, glances up to make eye contact, and then dives down to take my cock deep into his throat. I clench my fists in the bedding and resist the urge to pump into his mouth, letting him control how deep he takes me for now.

"Oh, fuck, precious. You feel amazing." I gasp out my praise. I reach for him, stroking his face reverently as he goes down on me like I'm the best thing he's ever put in his mouth. His wanton moaning zings along my cock, adding another layer of mind-blowing stimulation.

Tate has me on the edge of an orgasm in record time. The all-encompassing heat of his mouth sends rolling waves of pleasure through my nerves. The visual of my boy's head bobbing along my shaft is something straight out of my wildest fantasies. I can't imagine anything hotter than my precious boy gagging on my cock, except maybe if I was pounding into his ass. That might be a tossup. Either way, this is one of the sexiest moments of my life on so many levels, and I can't get enough of Tate.

CHAPTER 17

Tate

Sex with Rory, now that I know him, is even better than our first time together, when he was just a random guy I met over a broken toilet. This time, I know the man holding me tight. He's sweet and thoughtful and he makes me laugh.

Last night, in the tub, his hands moved over my body like I'm his most precious treasure. His touch is just as reverent now as he cups my cheek while he's resisting the urge to shove his cock balls deep into my throat. He turns me on so much.

My dick is achingly hard within the confines of my overnight diaper. The soft material hugs my ass. The waistband digs into my hips as my erection tries to poke out the top. Rory snapped them up tight enough that I can't really work a hand into them to touch myself.

The delicious sense of confinement and knowing daddy put me in this predicament has me all hot and bothered. I can't resist grinding against the bedding that's bunched under my body, trying to get desperately needed friction while I suck off my daddy. It's nowhere near enough, but that only makes me grind harder.

"Oh, so good." Rory gasps when I suck harder near the base of his cock. He bucks his hips before stilling them again when I swallow around his cockhead. "Just like that, I'm going to come." Rory warns me. And that is totally the point, so I repeat the move, adding a moan to amp up the stimulation and hopefully tip him over the edge. "Yes, Tate. Fuck. Yes." Daddy groans and thrusts into my mouth as he comes, his hand still on my jaw, stroking me lovingly even as he uses my mouth.

I take him as deep as I can, swallowing and suckling on his length until I need to come up for air. I tap his leg and he pulls out to let me catch my breath. His breathing is just as ragged as mine for a minute as he comes down from his orgasm. I kiss his shaft once more, and then Daddy pulls me up into a lip lock that has me harder than ever in my diaper. I shift to hump against him, and Daddy chuckles.

"Is my little boy still horny?" he teases.

I nod and hump into him again.

"Hm. Do you need Daddy to take care of your cock, precious?"

I nod and grind forward some more.

"Ask for it, precious."

"I need my daddy to take care of my little cock. Please? It's so hard it aches, Daddy."

"Ah, it hurts? Do you want me to kiss it better?"

"Yes, please." I nod emphatically. "I need you."

"Well then, I won't keep you waiting." Daddy chuckles as he nudges me off his lap. He lays me down on my back and strips me out of the soft fabric of my new pajama pants. He pulls them down to my ankles, revealing the penguin diaper from last night. For a moment, I feel awkward at having my lover strip me down to my cartoon print diaper. Custom ordered because they don't mass produce these in adult sizes.

I'm not used to letting my lovers see my little side. The two just don't mix for me, most of the time. But Rory doesn't miss a beat. He rubs my hard dick through the waterproof shell and presses his lips to my bulge, kissing me through the fabric like it's nothing out of the ordinary.

That makes it easier to accept that he's here for all of me. Tate the man and Tate, his precious little boy. Rory can handle being my daddy and my lover. The two roles don't have to stay in separate columns all the time. Sometimes the tenderness I need from my daddy can bleed over into my lover's touch.

I shiver as he pulls the snaps loose and folds the unused diaper open to free my dick.

"Nice and dry still, hmm? Such a big boy. You want me to kiss you here?" Daddy grips my cock gently.

"Yes, Daddy." I nod, clenching my hands in the bedding to keep from reaching for him and interfering in whatever he's about to do with me. He licks over my tip, teasing me with gentle licks and kisses when I want to be surrounded by him, consumed in his passion.

"You like that?" Daddy asks, torturing me with the interruption. I throw my head back and whine.

"More," I beg, beyond any ability to cover just how much I want him to wrap his lips around me and suck me for real. "Please, ungh, yes!" I hiss the last word as his tongue teases my slit and then delves around my foreskin. "Oh, heck. Yeah, there." I press his face against my dick. The sensation is too much and nowhere near enough at the same time. "No, don't stop!" I gasp when he lifts off of my dick to look up at me.

"You want to come in my mouth, precious? Let Daddy take care of you, just like you took care of me?"

I moan at the titles. Hearing him call me by my special nickname makes me all shivery. I've fantasized about letting my daddy make love to me, but until Rory, taking that step hasn't felt right. Not even when I wasn't little. It was just too intimate to share. But with Rory, it fits. I want him to take care of me, in and out of bed. He's not just my daddy when he's tucking me in and reading me bedtime stories.

He's Daddy when he texts me first thing in the morning to let me know he's thinking of me. And when he reminds me to stop for lunch despite my hectic work schedule. He's Daddy when he picks up treats for me while he shops for groceries. When he stocks his home with all things penguin, to make me smile.

He's Daddy when I wake up next to him, my boner achingly hard in the diaper that he fastened into place. And when we share our most intimate secrets. He's sweet and thoughtful all the time. Rory is exactly who I want. I want to call him my daddy all the time. Not just when he takes care of me, because it's not about what he does, it's about how he cares for me.

Daddy loves me, even if we haven't said it in so many words. He shows me with his actions, taking this slow as he licks and suckles and cherishes my dick with the same tender care he's given me in a million small ways for months.

I love him. Sex can't really change that. Not when it's just another way of expressing what we already feel for each other. One of many. And I seem to recall him mentioning something about back-to-back orgasms.

"Want to suck you again, too. Have you in my mouth while you suck me. Please, Daddy?" I beg.

Daddy moans agreeably around my cock, then he pulls off to rearrange. I whine a protest at the loss of contact. "Ugh, Daddy!"

"One second, precious." He shifts around so that he's kneeling astride my face. He reaches around to pump his erection back to standing, then hovers over me with his elbows braced on either side of my hips. I angle his glans between my lips even as he takes me back into his mouth again.

When I finally get his hard cock past my lips, I'm glad we agreed to do this skin-to-skin. He tastes good. Musky and wonderful and I love having him in my mouth, knowing that it's him. I've always found sucking on a guy soothing. It's not necessarily about making him come, either. I just like being stuffed full like this.

Sometimes I get so lost in having a thick shaft stretching my lips and filling my mouth up just right that I struggle to get my partner off this way. I love the weight of him on my tongue. It's like I was made to hold him here, cradle his most sensitive parts inside of me and give him pleasure. There's just something so fulfilling about being connected to him like this.

I find myself mouthing along his length and moaning as he takes me apart with his skilled tongue on my dick. He fondles my balls, and I can't help pumping my hips. He grips me more firmly, holding me still even as he dives down to take me deep in his throat. I don't stand a chance at holding back my orgasm when he swallows around my dick.

I garble out a warning, trying to pull out, but Daddy firms his grip on my ass, squeezing my butt cheeks and spreading them apart. He sucks more insistently and I shoot my load down his throat with a strangled cry around the dick in my mouth. The bitter tang of his pre-cum spreads over my tongue as I buck into his mouth.

Rory's pleasure is blending with my own and I can't separate the two sensations. It seems as though if I just keep sucking on him, the waves of my own pleasure will continue to roll over me indefinitely. I'm pretty sure he comes, too. For a drawn out moment, it's like I can freeze time and just live in the bliss of coming and making him come. I'd happily stay under him with his cock in my mouth all day if he let me. Even if there weren't orgasms involved.

The cool air on my dick when it slips from between his lips makes me whimper and suckle more insistently on his shaft. Rory presses a kiss to my cockhead and reaches down to ease himself out of my mouth. "It's a bit sensitive, precious, I need you to stop for now."

I reluctantly let him go. Daddy tucks himself away. He gets up and grabs a pair of my cartoon print briefs from my bag. "You ready to put on your big boy undies?"

"Help me?" I lift my legs for him to slide them into place.

"Up." He pats my thigh to get me to lift my hips to tug the waistband into place. Then he settles back on the bed and leans against his pillows. He opens his arms to me. "Come snuggle?"

I crawl up the bed and into his arms. "Thank you, Daddy. I like when you take care of me."

"Anytime, precious. You like having a dick to suck on, huh?"

There's no sense in denying the obvious. "Yep."

"Would you want to keep Daddy's cock nice and warm for me, next time we have a movie night?"

I glance at him and nod. "Yeah. Could I suck on you like a paci?"

"Sure, if that's something you'd want. It's not too much?"

"Nope. I'm ready to take this further with you. Can we do it soon? And get tested?"

"Sure, little one. We can go tomorrow, if we can get in for an appointment."

"I know a place that does same day testing." I look for my phone to check the availability.

Daddy grabs my wrist to stop me from lunging for it on the dresser. "You can look it up later. Right now, it's breakfast time."

"I already had my morning protein, Daddy. Can't we snuggle instead?" I pout, but my tummy rumbles, dashing my chances of more sleepy snuggles for now.

"Your tummy is all rumbly." Daddy wiggles his fingers at my

belly, giving me a gentle tickle to banish my post-sex lethargy. "We better feed it before the growly monster comes out." His fingers skating along my ribs make me giggle and squirm. "You ready to eat?" He pauses the tickle attack to let me get out of bed. I stay right where I am, lazy and contented in nothing but my undies and a light PJ shirt.

"What would you do if I turned into a growly monster?" I ask. I know not listening to Daddy means he's going to tickle me again, so I scrunch into a ball to be ready for his wiggly fingers. When he doesn't start to tickle me immediately, I tip my head back to watch him, and to tempt him with an easy target.

"Well..." Daddy presses a finger to his lips, like he's thinking hard about the answer. "I guess I'd have no choice but to tickle my little monster into submission." He waits a beat, giving me a chance to object. When I stay right where I am, he launches into tickling me.

Daddy worms his fingers into my armpits. I don't even try to hold in my shrieks of laughter, I just wriggle and writhe and laugh until tears drip down my cheeks and my belly hurts from laughing.

"Daddy! Stop! Tickles too much!" I cry out, loving that he isn't stopping. That he wants to be silly with me. Even though I'm bigger than him, he can make me feel small. His forceful grip when he moves me around feels like he could overpower me if he cared to. And that he cherishes me too much to ever use that power to hurt me. I roll to wrench away from his hands, and clench my elbows to my sides, pressing too tight to let him get back at my pits. In return, Daddy shifts his attention to the crook of my neck and my belly.

"What color is my little monster?" Daddy asks, not stopping the onslaught.

"Green," I force out through my laughter. "Green, green, green." I continue to roll around on the bed with Daddy tickling me until my tummy rumbles even louder and Daddy pins me down to blow raspberries on it. I laugh harder, stomach aching from the force of it, and curl around his face to try to get him to stop. "Enough, okay, we can eat now," I gasp.

Daddy stops tickling and scoops me into his arms to kiss all over my face and wipe away my tears. "My hungry little monster needs his breakfast. You ready to wash up?"

"Yes, Daddy." I nod. He pats my butt gently and I take it as my cue to get up and go to the washroom to pee and wash my hands. Daddy is a stickler about hand washing before meals. He goes to the kitchen and leaves me to get ready on my own. We have plenty of time to play more later.

CHAPTER 18

Tate

L ater the next week, I receive a message from my doctor's office that my latest test results are available in my patient portal. Of course, it arrives when I'm driving between job sites. My phone reads the subject line aloud for me. There's no way I can navigate to the actual patient portal hands free. Antsy as I am for the results, I wait until I find parking outside my next client's building to pull up the page.

Once I find a spot to stop, deciphering the rows of medical jargon to find the relevant results is an exercise in frustration. I give up reading every line in favor of skimming the page. The program hasn't highlighted any of the numbers in the bold font the office uses for test results that fall outside the healthy ranges. Like when I forgot to fast before my last physical, and my blood sugar came back super high from the donut I scarfed down right before the test.

Deep breath. I think the section with the STI panel all reads as negative. Which means we can put aside that last barrier between us tonight, bond in a way I've never been with anyone before. That's assuming he also got his results. He should have. We got our bloodwork drawn the same day, after we spent most of last Sunday morning in bed making love.

I screenshot the results and text them to Daddy. A few minutes later, as I'm gathering up my tools to go inside, my phone rings. I smile to myself as I answer.

"Hi, Daddy, did you see what came?"

"Your test results. I'm pulling up the patient portal now for my lab results." Rory's voice sounds muffled as he switches to speakerphone to pull up his profile.

"Yep. If I'm interpreting the results correctly, you know what else can come?"

"What?" Daddy asks.

"Your dick. In my ass."

"Remind me about the rules for teasing Daddy when we can't actually do anything?"

"Hm, was that a rule?" I tease.

"You want to suck me tonight, or do you want to have some corner time instead?" He asks in his growly 'I mean business' voice. Too bad for him; I'm on to the fact that he's a giant softie.

"Fine, I'll be good. But can I have your dick inside me tonight?"

"Sure, precious. If that's what you want, I'm good with it." The sounds of him doing something on the computer filter through the receiver. "Ah, I had to reset my password, but I'm in now. Looks like my little boy is getting his wish. I'll send you a screenshot with my results, too, okay?"

"Okay. Thanks, Daddy. I'll see you after work?" I shift my phone from one ear to the other.

"Yep. I'll let you go for now. The sooner you finish fondling other people's ballcocks, the sooner you can come home and slobber all over my cock and balls."

I bite back a moan at the thought. "I rarely fondle ballcocks at work, Daddy."

"Oh yeah, is that because of the rise in DIY ballcock handling?" Daddy teases.

"Nope." I grunt as I heft up my toolbox. "It's because most

toilets use newer designs these days. It's tragic, really, one less filthy work joke just ripe for the plucking."

"Ah, well, I'd try another terrible pun for your amusement, but I've plumbed the depths of my plumbing knowledge."

"I'll plumb your depths if you keep trying to tease me at work. That rule should work both ways, Daddy."

"I am so on board for that. The sex part, not the little boys making the rules part."

"Yeah? Cool, I already told you I'm vers, so, whatever you want. I prefer to bottom, though."

"And I prefer topping most of the time, so that works out for us both."

"Yeah it does." I grin, already anticipating tonight. "Guess I'll stop at home to get myself ready before our date."

"Can't wait."

"Me neither. But for now, I'm headed in to meet with a client, so I'll talk to you later."

We say goodbye and I spend the rest of my workday half-hard every time my mind turns toward what awaits me tonight. I've spent most of the past week sleeping over at his place since we agreed to have sex. Nightly orgasms with my daddy ought to make it easier to ignore my dick at work, but sex with Rory is one of my new favorite things.

It takes all my professionalism and self-discipline to get through the rest of my day. I've never struggled so hard to sit still and focus on recording the days' invoices to send to Luke. It gives me a flash of sympathy for Monty and his issues with maintaining focus. It's a relief when I hit send and call Luke for our nightly check-in, since that's my last work task of the day.

"You're still coming over, right? I know the Fling might

make for a late night, so no pressure." Luke ends our chat by confirming that I'm coming over for dinner with Monty and him this weekend. I almost ask if I can bring Rory, but one new partner at dinner seems less daunting. It's nice to have the air cleared with Luke so there aren't secrets between us, though. I'm glad I confronted him about his obvious sneaking around with Monty earlier this week. I want to introduce him to Rory soon. Maybe even at the club this weekend if the timing seems right.

"Are you kidding? I'll be there. We can celebrate you making things with Monty public and official."

"At least one of us is confident he'll say yes to me," Luke says wryly.

"Are you kidding me? He's head over heels for you, bro. Don't even worry about it. If you ask him to be with you forever, Monty will say yes." That's absolutely true. Monty might not have felt comfortable sharing his new relationship with me, but I know him. And I've never seen him be this into someone he's dating.

"Yeah?" Luke asks, all wistful and practically begging for reassurance. That vulnerable note in his voice isn't characteristic of him. It reminds me of when we were younger and he needed me to comfort him. Back when we were figuring out how to be brothers to each other after our moms first got married. That emotional openness convinces me more than ever that he and Monty are for real. He hasn't let himself fall this hard in a long time. Maybe not ever.

"One hundred percent. You're it for him, so don't fuck it up. Got me?" I tease.

"Yeah. I've got you. Speaking of, what have *you* been up to all summer? Monty said he hasn't seen nearly as much of anyone from your usual gang for months."

I snort. "Yeah, well, your lovebird skipped out on half our hangouts. I've at least been going to Q and Kylee's parties. Unlike certain lovestruck boys."

"So, you're good?"

"Yeah, Luke. I'm more than good. Might have someone to introduce you to soon, too. We're just taking things slow."

"Because, Gary?" Luke is immediately sympathetic about the number my ex did on my trust.

"No. I mean, at first, yeah," I admit. "But now it's mostly because he's sweet and I'm having fun getting to know him slowly, drawing out the anticipation has been fun. Although I might be ready to move things along." I clear my throat meaningfully.

Luke chuckles. "Am I keeping my baby brother from getting laid? Should we finish this chat tomorrow?"

I laugh along with him. "No comment? I'll send over the nightly invoices before I head to his place. But, yeah. Don't tell Monty yet? I don't want to take away from your spotlight this weekend. We'll have you and him over later, okay?" I crush the pang of guilt at not telling my best friend about my boyfriend yet. He's still keeping the fact he's dating Luke from me. And I want to be the one to tell him about Rory, in person. Soon. I just hope he won't be upset that I didn't tell him sooner. I meant to, but then he got all cagey about the guy he was seeing and we stopped talking about our love lives.

"Deal. We'll set up a double date whenever you're ready for us to meet your man. Just do it soon. Monty will be happy for you." It's Luke's turn to reassure me. He's good at reading people. "Is he your daddy?"

"Duh."

"Good for you. I'm happy you found someone who makes you as happy as Monty makes me, Tatey-Tot."

"Thanks, Lucas." We wrap up the call after that. Then I slog through my remaining work tasks. I shut down my computer with enough time to take a thorough shower before I head over to Daddy's place.

Daddy greets me at his door with a kiss. I cling to him, grabbing at his ass and pressing my hard bulge against him until he nudges me away. "Hello to you, too." He grins at me, his eyes traveling along my body, so I'm pretty sure he isn't saying 'no', so much as 'not in my entryway.'

"Hi, Daddy." I give him a cheeky wave, then make myself at home, toeing off my shoes and wandering into the living room where Daddy keeps all my toys stashed. The fact I have little stuff all over his apartment, stuff that he bought just for me, makes the giddy feeling in my chest expand. He's everything I want. I turn to face Daddy, dropping my overnight bag by the couch.

"You want to eat first?" He asks me, quirking up a brow in question.

"Nope, unless you're offering me your tasty meat?" I step into his personal space. Rory standing there in his loungewear is sexy as fuck, and I don't have to resist him a moment longer. I want to blow him so badly I can practically taste him. I brush my fingers over his bulge to emphasize the clumsy innuendo.

Daddy snorts in amusement as he grips my wrist to press my hand more firmly against his crotch. "Yeah, I paid a premium for this sausage, so let's go easy on the eating talk, hmm?"

I stroke his length, and he presses into my palm. I have a weird moment of disconnect between the flaccid dick in my hand and the way he moans at my touch. But then Daddy kisses me again, full of passion. The moment passes. He's as into this as I am, regardless of hardness.

Daddy reaches into his pants to pump up his cock. Good, I like him hard. "Yeah, okay. I'll be so gentle. I just want you in my mouth. And in my ass."

"Come here, then." Daddy crowds me toward the couch. He sits, knees spread wide, and tosses a throw pillow onto the carpet between his feet. I catch his meaning and kneel on it, watching greedily as Daddy pulls his thick dick out of his pants and strokes himself. He gets harder as he plays with his balls, which makes me smile about his silly attempt at a plumbing joke earlier all over again. A soft chuckle escapes me.

"What?" Daddy asks, amused.

"Nothing." I lick my lips. "Just wondering if you want to DIY that ballcock or let the professional handle it."

"Professional, huh?" Daddy points his dick toward me. "Well?"

So I lean forward and take him into my mouth, moaning at the salty smoothness of his skin against my tongue. It's not my first time blowing him, but there is something about knowing he's going to fuck me with it—nothing between us—that makes this more intense.

I never want to stop being able to do this with him. Daddy lets me explore the head of his dick with my tongue, tracing along the glans and dipping into the moist slit at the tip. He tastes like pre-cum, which I wasn't entirely expecting the first time he let me blow him, but I like it. I chase more of his sweet muskiness until he urges me to open and take him further into my mouth. His breath quickens and his fingers on my shoulders squeeze tight with pleasure-soaked urgency.

"That's it, Tate, take every inch of me." Daddy strokes the back of my head, nudging me to take him deeper. I bob along his length, relaxing my throat to let him slide in and out. He moans, the sounds of his pleasure are as much an encouragement as his dirty talk. I want to take him all the way inside of me. I want to pleasure him as well as he always takes care of me. Not just sexually, either.

When I'm with him, I never have to hide any part of myself

and getting to experience him in this way is wonderful. I swirl my tongue around his head again when I pull back, before diving down to suck him all the way into my throat. I take my time working him deeper with every stroke of my mouth along his length. Once he's seated as deep as he can go, I swallow around him, drawing a groan of pleasure.

"Oh, that's so fucking good, precious. Get it nice and wet for your pretty little hole." Daddy strokes my throat, like he can feel himself there, the way he stretches me and makes me his. I pump the base of his dick with a firm grip, stroking him the way he likes while taking his shaft as far down my throat as I can handle.

He's getting close to the tipping point, breathing ragged, hips lifting to meet my every move. I breathe into this new rhythm, imagining that he's connected to me on a primal level, tangled up in me. As if the motion of his cock in and out controls the tide of my breathing and the beat of my heart.

"Oh, fuck. Tate. So, good. Need to be inside you, precious, get up here." I'm only vaguely aware of him warning me he's about to blow. I don't want to pull off, but he asked me to stop, so I let him slip free of my mouth. Gazing up at him, I lick my lips. Daddy leans down and crashes his mouth against mine in a hard kiss that's all lust and need. The angle is awkward, and I am so hard it hurts, so I scramble up into his lap to continue making out.

"Fuck, Tate." Daddy gasps for breath. His hands grip my shoulders hard, like he needs to anchor himself. "My precious boy." He urges me up to my feet. I hastily strip off my pants so I can straddle him properly, hands balanced on his shoulders as I kneel up over him and reach for his cock. I lubed up and prepped before I came over. So I line up his spit-slick tip with my hole and slowly, ever-so-slowly, lower myself down onto his shaft.

Daddy grabs my ass and squeezes hard, urging me to take him

deeper, but I draw it out, teasing us both with the slow slide into pleasure. He claims my mouth in another passionate kiss. Our lips seal together, made for each other. I open, letting him taste himself on my tongue. We both moan as I finally lower all the way down, taking him to the root. I grind my ass back against his thighs, then forward. Each glide rubs my hard-on against him. Daddy wraps his hand around my shaft to stroke me while I ride him without breaking the kiss.

Daddy jerks me off, his tongue fucking into my mouth and chasing every trace of himself. It all makes me feel so wanton. Like I'm a horny teenager staring at a smutty image from a magazine while I hump my own fist and try to imagine someone else touching me. Another guy holding me in his lap like this while he plows up into my ass has long been a favorite fantasy. The reality of being held close and allowed to let loose lives up to my imagination and then some.

It's even better when his breathing gets ragged as he approaches the edge. Daddy stops letting me control the ride, wrapping an arm around me to hold me in place while he thrusts up into me, taking his pleasure. It doesn't take long for me to be right on the edge. His fist squeezes tight while his dick massages my prostate with every stilted roll of my hips and I have to fight not to come yet.

Daddy jerks me off with one hand while his other hand digs into my ass cheek. His grip kneading me adds an extra bit of stretch and pins me more firmly in place as he claims every part of me. I shudder as the orgasm creeps up on me, and then I'm clenching tight around him as he takes over completely. Daddy thrusts up into me in hard, sharp jabs that get us both over the finish line in a frantic rush.

Daddy doesn't stop jerking me until I whimper into his mouth and squirm to get free of the overstimulation. "Too much, Daddy." I whine.

He releases my dick, shifts to ease his dick out of my ass, and peers down at me. "Sorry, precious, did Daddy make my boy feel good?"

"So good." I nod, then drape my arms around his neck to keep him close. "I really liked that. Blowing you and riding you while you held me tight."

"I could tell." Daddy holds up his sticky hand, my cum dripping over his palm to his wrist in clear evidence of my pleasure. On an impulse, I grab his hand and suck his fingers into my mouth to clean him. Daddy closes his eyes and moans at the suction. Yeah, I know that sensation of something unrelated going right to my cock.

"Greedy little boy," Daddy teases when I move on to his next finger, sucking each clean and then lapping over his hand to get the last of the mess.

"Yep." I agree proudly. "I'll always be greedy for you, Daddy."

"Well, if you're that hungry, I think we should fill up your belly with some actual food before I let you have another mouthful of my dick."

I pretend to consider, so he tickles my ribs. "Hm, nope, still just want you in my mouth, Daddy."

"We'll just see about that. My hungry boy needs his healthy dinner before he gets to have more treats." He redoubles the tickle torture until I squirm right off his lap and onto the cushion beside him.

"No!" I writhe to protect my most sensitive bits. "Please, Daddy, don't let the tickle monster gobble me up!"

I clench my elbows tight to my sides and rock side to side beneath him. He doesn't let up until I gasp out a concession. "Okay, yellow, we can eat, we can eat!" Daddy stops as soon as I say yellow.

"You good?" He checks, offering me a hand to rise. I let him haul me to my feet with an oomph.

"Yeah, I have to pee, though." I consider trying to tickle him back, but my tummy rumbles, reminding me it's been a long time since the toast I gobbled down on my morning commute. And I really need to pee. I shuffle my feet.

"Let me wash up, and then you can go to the bathroom while I get dinner heated for us, precious."

"Thanks, Daddy." I kiss his cheek, then head for the washroom.

CHAPTER 19

Rory

I watch Tate's bare backside sway as he goes to the bathroom before supper. He's always adorable. Tonight is no different. Still, I've never seen anything hotter than my precious boy straddling my lap, impaled on my hard cock while he came, his defenses all down. He trusted me, and that's priceless. So is knowing that we can play and be silly after coming our brains out together.

I'm glad we waited to bring sex into things. And even more glad that we waited to make going bare something special. A moment of bonding that meant the world to me. Fluid exchanges might be a casual thing for some people, but for me, it means something. And considering how careful Tate is about mixing kink and sex, I think it meant just as much to him.

That I'm his and he is mine. What we just did is a symbolic way of carrying a piece of him around with me, come what may. He was so eager to get his mouth on me and I've got plans to keep up the intimacy after dinner, too. But first my hungry boy probably skipped lunch again, so I'm going to make sure he eats a healthy dinner.

After eating and a bit of playtime in the living room, I declare that it's bath time. Once I sponge him clean, Tate splashes until his fingers are wrinkly and the warm water has gone tepid. That's our cue to put away his bath toys.

I wrap Tate in a fluffy towel, then bundle my clean boy into his diaper and pajamas. Getting to take care of him this way is still new. I love this part of our bedtime routine now that he's staying over some night. There is nothing quite like the naked trust in his eyes when he gazes up at me while I wrap his soft diaper around him. Or when I change him out of it in the morning.

His growing comfort level with wearing a diaper around my home this past week is one of those details that reinforces how deep the bond between us runs. It gives me a rush every time he turns his toileting needs over to me like this. He only rarely uses the diaper before having me change him, but it still means the world that he's giving me this much control and trust. More often than not, I use his wipes to clean the cum off his cock after he rubs off against me to relieve his sleepy morning wood.

Tonight, it's still early enough that I suggest cuddles and a movie before bed. Tate agrees and we settle on the couch together with my boy sprawled across the cushion next to me. I let him pick the movie and hit play. Tate squirms around until the first musical number. He bops along to the beat, then cuddles into my side when the song ends.

I settle an arm around him. He snuggles closer, sliding down my side until his head is in my lap as he sucks his thumb. I card my fingers through his hair. He nuzzles against my bulge, making it all too easy to imagine his hot mouth sucking on me instead. I adjust myself. Tate twists to flash me a coy little grin around his thumb.

"Did you want something?" I ask, totally failing at sounding stern.

Tate points at my dick without removing his thumb from his mouth.

"You want to use Daddy like a paci?" I suggest. As soon as the words are out, I know that's what he wants and I want it too. I love having his mouth on me when we're fucking, but this is something different. It's about closeness and sharing comfort. Being skin to skin and giving each other a bit of tenderness that we both crave.

He nods.

"Can you say please?"

"Please?" Tate repeats, the word garbled from having his thumb still in his mouth, though he's not really sucking at the moment.

"Go ahead." I reach to unfasten my pants and pull out my flaccid dick. Tate shifts his body so that he can lie comfortably facing toward me, then he slurps my cock into his mouth and holds me there. I clench up to resist the initial urge to push in deeper. I have to count to ten to remind myself this isn't about getting off, it's about our connection.

Even with no sexual intent, Tate's mouth feels good. A warm embrace for my dick that I never want to leave. Every so often, he sucks a little before resting his soft tongue against me and just holding me again. Cradling my dick inside of him like I'm as precious to him as he is to me.

Neither of us is really watching the movie, but I don't turn it off. Tate takes one of my hands and squeezes. I stroke his face with the other and murmur praise to him. "Such a good boy for your daddy, precious."

Tate makes a contented little noise in his throat, suckles, and then nuzzles his forehead into my belly.

"That's my precious boy. You want to keep your daddy warm and cozy until bedtime?"

"Mhm," Tate tips his head in an abbreviated nod, the movement small to keep from jostling me too much. The vibrations of his reply have me fighting back another jolt of pleasure. What this boy does to me is incredible. It's just as well that I can control whether and when I get hard. I seem to be a perfect mouthful for him as it is, and I don't want him to have a sore jaw later. Tate warms my cock until the final credits roll on the screen and I urge him to let me pull out of his mouth.

He grimaces and wipes drool off his lips and chin, working his jaw a bit.

"Are you sore?"

"No." Tate pouts. "Can I have my paci back?"

"You want to sleep with Daddy's special paci in your mouth, precious?"

"No, but I enjoy tasting you. You fit just right."

"I'm all yours. You can put me in your mouth whenever you need something to suck on while we're playing. But it's bedtime now, okay?"

"Okay, Daddy." Tate stretches and yawns. I help him off the couch and he trudges sleepily into my room.

Tate rouses enough to dig both of his penguin stuffies out of his bag. He tucks them in on his side of the bed before crawling across the mattress to sit in my lap. Someday soon, I hope that might be their permanent spot. I want him in my bed every night. I've had a summer full of taking things slow and I'm ready for more of him. Ready to be reckless and invite my little boy to share my life.

I reach for Tate's favorite penguin book before I can blurt out an invitation for him to move in with me. I'm planning on giving him a key, so he can come and go as he pleases. Would it be too much to ask him to move in now?

Tate snuggles into my arms for his story. Not even my silliest voices keep him from falling asleep before we get to the last page. I set aside the book and turn out the lights. The movement jostles my sleepy boy, and he mumbles a protest.

"Sorry, precious, go back to bed." I shift to spoon against him and hold him tight.

"Night, Daddy. Love you." Tate's words are barely audible. I freeze up at that phrase. I know he's more than half asleep when he says those three little words, but I'm pretty sure he means them. Even if they only slipped out because he's more asleep than awake and his defenses are down. We've danced around it before, but he hasn't actually said those exact words to me yet. Whether or not he meant to say it like this, the words fill something inside me, like water on parched ground and I can't help saying them back to him. I've felt this for a while now.

"I love you too, Tate," I whisper into his nape, unable to hold back any longer.

"Mhm. It's cuz I'm so lovable." Tate surprises me by replying.

My boy might not be as sleepy as I'd thought, but I don't regret saying it to him like this. He pulls my arm more securely around himself and scoots his butt back against my groin. I take the hint to hold him tight, breathing in the clean, soapy scent of him.

It might not have been a dramatic declaration, but then again, I don't think either of us needs a big production. We just needed to say the words. And I have every intention of telling him over and over for as long as he'll let me. Once I give him a key to my place, hopefully I'll be able to tell him in person every night before bed. With Tate in my arms, I fall asleep, thanking my lucky stars that the universe brought me to him, my perfect boy.

CHAPTER 20

Tate

I t's hard to believe Adventures is open again after the long summer without my favorite gathering place. The Summer Fling is always one of the club's most popular events, but it's even more packed than usual since it's also the grand reopening this year. Pretty much everyone I know is planning to attend. I meet up with Monty early in the evening.

Martin gave Daddy a guest pass to come tonight. He had to record today, so we agreed to meet here. I anxiously scan the crowd for him. Monty appears too preoccupied with his own thoughts to remark upon my inattention. He flits from one topic to the next, as usual. Crowds make it harder for him to focus, so I don't take his distractibility personally.

We check out all the upgrades together for the first part of the evening. Then Martin introduces us to his new boy, Bobby. That's when Monty catches sight of Luke perusing the new suspension rig. He lights up like a kid on a sugar rush, and I've lost any claim on his attention. With barely a rushed goodbye to us, he makes his way across the room.

I watch him go, and judging from the way my bestie gloms onto my brother, I won't be seeing him again tonight. I'm sure they'll be off to one of the private rooms ASAP. Monty goes a step further, kissing Luke in front of anyone who cares to watch. It won't be long before the entire club knows Luke is Monty's daddy. The thought makes me smile.

I don't dwell on Monty for long, though. Martin plays with a lot of partners, but I've never seen him look at anyone the way he looks at Bobby. He also doesn't usually lavish casual touches on a partner outside of a scene the way he does with Bobby.

"You and the others still have that monthly D&D game, right?" Martin asks, drawing my full attention back to him. Bobby perks up at the mention.

"We do." I nod, already suspecting where this conversation is headed.

"My Bobby is a big fan, aren't you, boy?" Martin gives the boy a friendly nudge.

"Yeah. Just kind of broke up with my regular group over the summer. We lost our DM, and they wanted me to take over, but it made me realize that we'd drifted apart. So, I'm between groups for now."

"That stinks. We could probably fit in another player. Harry, our DM, isn't kinky, but the rest of the group is here. Want me to introduce you around?"

Bobby gives Martin a look that says he's not sure if he needs permission to agree, but he wants it regardless. Martin might not be a daddy dom, but I know how invested he is in taking care of people he feels responsible for. If he and Bobby are together, I suspect Bobby will fit in with my friends.

For the moment, I give up on scanning the crowd for Daddy, and take Bobby's hand to introduce him to Connor and Quent. My friends should be easier to find than Daddy, if only because I know for sure that they're both here.

Sure enough, I catch Q's eye from across the room. They tip their head toward the raised stage where Monty and Luke are still standing too close to be casual and raise a brow. They want my reaction to the relationship between my brother and my best friend. I give an exaggerated shrug, since I just want them to be happy.

"Hey! Did you know about Luke and Monty?" Q asks as soon as I reach them. Bobby stands off to the side uncertainly. Quent gives me a bone-creaking hug. Connor gives me a more subdued clap on the back.

"Hey, you two. This is Bobby." I make perfunctory introductions. Quent and Connor reciprocate.

"Hi, Bobby. So, did you know about Monty?" Q presses me.

"I figured it out, yeah. Monty still hasn't said anything. When I asked Luke about it, he said Monty didn't trust it to last," I say.

Connor nods, his smile turning sad. "That sounds like Monty. Luke told you that was crap, right?"

"Yeah, he agrees Monty is a catch. I suspect he has a romantic gesture planned. Although, I think that display of affection on the main stage is probably enough of an announcement, huh?" I chuckle.

"So long as Luke didn't give him a reason to think he needed to hide, or that he was ashamed of our boy," Q narrows their eyes.

"Nothing like that. I think keeping it quiet was Monty's way of protecting himself. Either way, I've got a dinner date planned with them both for the obligatory brother slash best friend 'if you hurt him, I'm coming for you.' talk." I wink.

"Good." Connor and Q nod their approval.

"So, you're cool with it?" Q checks.

"Yep. Happy that they're both happy. Hopefully, we'll see more of Monty now that the club is open, and he isn't trying to hide his relationship."

"Here's hoping," Connor agrees.

"So, what do you think of Harry's handiwork?" Q asks, bouncing back to upbeat now that we've covered Monty's juicy gossip.

"The club looks great. We'll have to bring Harry cookies for our next D&D session," I say, and then remember why I came over to see them. "Have you both met Bobby?" I ask, abashedly turning to include the new boy in our conversation.

"Yep, Martin brought him to hang out with Mommy and me." Q waves. "How've you been? Sorry to ignore you there, Monty's one of our besties, so we've been speculating about who his hot summer hookup is for months."

"I'm good. I can appreciate prioritizing juicy gossip," he says dryly. That sense of humor reminds me of Martin, and I can see where they might be a good fit.

"Right? It turned out to be his bestie's brother." Q nods solemnly. "Too bad my brother is happily married, or I'd take a page from Monty's book and hook you up with him, Con." Quent nudges Connor playfully.

"I'm good." Connor says shiftily, eyes tracking toward the far corner of the room. I follow his gaze to where Jax is photographing the event in his official capacity. That's interesting. Q picks up on where he's looking, too.

"Yeah, you are," Q agrees, looping an arm around Connor's shoulders.

"So, Martin said you all have a D&D group I might join." Bobby breaks back into the conversation.

"Oh! Yes. We do. The more the merrier, right?" Q turns belatedly to Connor and me to confirm we're on board with adding a new member to our tight-knit group.

"Right." Connor and I agree. It might be fun to introduce fresh blood to our campaign. And our party could use a healer since we all chose beat sticks that just rush into battle with minimal strategy most of the time. It's a lack Harry has bemoaned on multiple occasions. We manage fine, but none of us get too creative with advanced battle tactics or min-maxing our character builds into having wildly overpowered abilities.

Q asks Bobby about his play style and the four of us chat for a while longer about our campaign, our characters, and how often we play. Connor and I are both distracted, him watching Jax and me scanning the crowd for Rory's arrival. We make plans for Bobby to join us for our next game session. And Q makes oblique comments about wanting to get the gang together privately before the session to share some big cryptic news that I'm pretty sure Connor already knows.

Eventually, the others wander off and I go to peruse the refreshments as a distraction from my growing nerves that Daddy isn't here yet. His last-minute retakes are probably just running later than expected. And yet, a small part of me is afraid that we moved too fast this past week. What if he isn't ready to be my daddy in a big public venue? I quash that voice of doubt and go back to keep Connor company since he's still pining over Jax. Maybe he'll want to talk about whatever is going on between the two of them. That might distract me from my worries over what's taking Rory so long.

CHAPTER 21

Rory

After spending the past few months getting into a groove with Tate, going to the grand reopening event at Adventures shouldn't be a big deal. It's not like when I first moved here and was trying to work up the courage to step into a kinky lifestyle and make new friends. I have friends. Sort of.

I've got Tate, anyway. And we've been to a few play parties at Kylee and Q's place over the summer. The big party where we first got to play together and several smaller ones. We also attended a couple of munches together, where I got to know Kylee and some other bigs and the pup handlers Kylee knows. One of whom is walking up to the entrance to the club as I arrive, Clark, if I recall correctly. I hold the door for him, relieved to have someone whose cue I can follow about how they do things here.

"Hey, thanks, Rory, right?" Clark asks.

"Yep. Good to see you again, Clark. No Niko tonight?" I ask after the pup he had with him the last time we met.

Clark guffaws. "It's Nicholas when he's not a pup, and he's already here, caught a ride over with one of his boyfriends."

"Oh. I thought you two..." I stumble over my words because I could have sworn I saw the pair of them sporting matching wedding bands at the munch where we met.

"We're married." Clark waggles his ringed finger at me. "And he dates other people. Works for us." He shrugs, all but daring me to say anything about it.

I smile at him. "Hey, whatever works for you guys. Don't suppose you can show me the ropes here?"

"Ropes aren't my thing, but I can point you toward one of our resident experts if it's yours." Clark winks at me, knowing that isn't what I meant. Before I can say as much, he claps a friendly hand on my shoulder. "Just playing with you, man. Here, I'll introduce you to Cathy. She runs the front desk and can take your phone if you brought one. No unauthorized recording devices allowed inside. There're lockers for anything else you don't want to keep on you or if you want to slip into a different outfit. You can rent a lock from Cathy, too. At least, that's how things were before the renovations. Let's see how much has changed. You aren't the only visitor here tonight, with the party going strong."

Clark sticks by my side as we wait in a short line composed of as many guests and visitors as regular club members, at least according to him. I turn over my phone and my guest pass, then sign some paperwork. Between Cathy, Clark, and reading up on the club's website, I feel confident of the rules for the night when we get inside the crowded public areas.

Clark sticks by my side, pointing out all the upgrades that Martin made over the summer and detailing the many features available in the private rooms. True to his word, he even points out the rigger he joked about introducing me to.

"That's Luke. He joined not too long ago, but he's been around the local scene for years. Check out his private workshops, if you really are interested in ropes."

I follow his pointing and do a double take. I recognize the man from Tate's social media profile. Luke. As in Tate's brother and business partner. And there's a boy wrapped around him. Long red hair pulled back in a distinctive ponytail.

Monty. Tate's best friend, whom I've only met twice at large gatherings. Well, if they were involved in some sort of secret relationship, that probably explains why Tate complained about not seeing as much of either of them this summer.

I wonder if my boy knows about the two of them yet. Thoughts of Tate have me scanning the crowd for my boy again when Nicholas and another young guy approach us.

"Daddy, you're early!" Nicholas wraps an arm around Clark and kisses him on the lips while his boyfriend watches.

"Got out of work a bit earlier than I expected," Clark explains when they step apart.

Nicholas angles himself toward the other man he's with, grinning broadly. "We were just going to see if the red room is available. Want to play with us?" Nicholas winks at his daddy.

"That depends. What do you say, Ethan?" Clark asks.

"The more the merrier, Daddy." Ethan winks at Clark.

Clark smirks. "I'll just show you merry." He hesitates and gives me a guilty look. "Will you be alright if I abandon you here?"

"Yeah, of course, have fun." I wave away his hospitality.

Ethan eyes me up and down, licking his lips suggestively. "I mean, you're welcome to join us, too. What was your name? I don't believe we've met." He offers me a handshake.

"Rory. And I should check in with my boy." I beg off from whatever the three of them have planned for the evening.

"Ah. Should have known all the hot daddies are always taken." Ethan pouts playfully. "Are you two exclusive?"

"We are." I put some distance between myself and the flirty boy.

Nicholas slugs him in the arm. "Come on Eth, you've got your hands full for the night already."

"Yeah. That better not be the only part of me that's full by the end of the night." He winks at me over his shoulder as Nicholas shepherds him toward one of the private rooms.

"That boy is a handful." Clark remarks with a broad smile. "I better not keep the two of them waiting. See you around, Rory."

"Yep, thanks for the tour." I flash him a smile.

Clark waves off my thanks and follows Nicholas and Ethan to the private room. Left to my own devices, I wander the large public area, taking in the crowd and the club's features. I can't see Tate, but I find Kylee and Q watching a mild spanking scene off in an alcove between two of the private rooms.

"Hi, Daddy Rory," Q greets me with a grin. They bounce toward me, leaving a respectful distance between our conversation and the duo they were watching. "Tate was looking for you earlier."

Kylee comes to join us at a more sedate pace. She rests a hand on Q's nape, settling their fidgety energy.

"Hello," I wave to both Q and Kylee. "I don't suppose you know where he might be?"

Q shrugs. "Last I saw him, he was chatting with Martin and Martin's new boy. Then he introduced Bobby to Con and me, to suggest Bobby might want to join our D&D campaign. He seemed distracted, but that was right after Monty practically tackle-hugged Luke in front of everyone. So that might be why? I totally called it that those two were a thing."

"I think we all saw that one coming," Kylee remarks dryly. "But it's still not polite to gossip, Quent."

"Sorry, Mommy. I'm just happy for them. Tate said he knew already." They glance toward the occupied spanking bench and bite their lip longingly. I follow their gaze to where the spanking they were watching is wrapping up with the top rubbing their bottom's ass cheeks and murmuring low in their ear.

Kylee clears her throat and gives Q a no-nonsense look. Q ducks their head sheepishly, but their smile is full of mischief when I catch their eye. Kylee is smiling, too, so that the disobedience comes across like a game. "Looks like my pup needs a reminder about wagging tongues. Again. If you'll excuse us, Rory?"

"Of course. I'll talk to you both later." I nod toward them.

"Bye, Rory. Tate's wearing his penguin footie PJs, if that helps you find him." Q gives me a cheeky wave before their mommy steers them toward the newly vacant spanking bench for whatever punishment she deems appropriate. Kylee leans in close to detail her plans for the pup, but her voice is too soft to carry over the ambient noise.

I don't stick around to watch. Sure, it's a public venue, and I could. They wouldn't be doing a scene out here if they didn't want an audience, but I'm too preoccupied with finding Tate to focus on anything else.

Did he know about his best friend and his brother getting together? He mentioned Monty and Luke acting weirdly evasive in conversations and not having as much free time to hang out with them this summer. But he'd mostly attributed the lack of time to a booming work schedule to where he's considering hiring another plumber or taking on an apprentice of his own. That and eking out as much time as he could to spend with me.

The only way to know how my boy is taking the news is to ask him. So I turn back toward the crowd with renewed purpose. I see Monty again, sitting astride Luke's lap on a couch near one of the private rooms. The two of them are making out like they're the only ones in the world.

And then I find Tate standing with Connor and Jackson. My

beautiful boy sees me at the same time. Our eyes lock from across the room. Tate turns, presumably to excuse himself from the other two, and then he's pushing his way through the crowd to get to me.

I skirt around a scene so as not to disturb the folks playing and make my way closer to him. We meet in the middle of an open patch of floor. Tate flings himself into my arms, hugging me tight.

"Daddy!" he squeals. "You're here!"

I kiss his temple and spin him in a circle. "Of course I'm here, precious. Wouldn't have missed it. I want everyone to know you're mine." And I kiss him full on the lips, claiming him as mine with an audience of our peers. Not that most of the other club patrons are paying us any attention, but it's the principle of the thing. When we break the kiss, Tate is breathless and clinging to me.

"I wasn't sure you were still coming," he admits.

"I wouldn't stand you up, Tate. Got held up, grabbing something for you after I finished at the studio." I fumble the spare key I had cut for him out of my pocket. The part that made me late was collecting the perfect little crochet penguin keychain that's dangling from the key. The intern who digitized my *Scamper* VHS tape makes them. I had to swing by his place to pick up my custom order along with the flash drive with the movie files on it.

"What's this little cutie for?" Tate sounds bemused as he takes the tiny blue penguin from me, not seeming to notice the key at first. When he does, his hand goes to his mouth. "Daddy?" he asks, as though he doesn't dare to believe the key means what he thinks it does.

"I had a spare key made for you. Since you've been staying over so much. And no pressure, but when you're ready, I want you to move in with me." I'd planned to ask him later. Over a private romantic dinner, but gazing into his eyes, I don't want to wait any longer to have him in my bed every night. To be the one bringing him his bottle and changing his diaper and holding him all night long. I want all the bath times, and bedtimes and playtimes and sexy times. I want Tate, and Fuzzy and Spot, to be permanent fixtures in my bed and my life.

Tate wraps both hands around my head and kisses me, his tongue delving into my mouth with all the fiery lust-fueled passion of our first hookup. When he comes up for air, he nods, tears shining in his eyes.

"Is that a yes?" I ask, since he hasn't actually answered me yet.

"Yes." Tate pulls me into another kiss, this time letting me control the tangling of our tongues. When we part, he adds, "I want to live with you, Daddy. I want everything with you." And then he's kissing me again, and I want nothing more than to have my boy in my arms.

CHAPTER 22

Tate

"Where does this one go?" Luke asks as he hefts the box that Monty covered in dick drawings and labeled as 'Tate's toys'. I told him it wasn't those types of toys, but no one has ever accused Monty of being discreet. And since I refused to show him which box has my sex toys in it, he went to town decorating that one.

"Living room," I say at the same time Daddy tries to take the box from my brother.

Daddy and Luke bump into each other. The box topples to the ground, dumping my action figures across the carpet. Apparently, Monty spiced up my toy drawer, because a massive neon yellow dildo I've never seen before rolls out at my feet, buzzing away.

"Daddy unleashed the bees!" Monty exclaims as he scoops the toy off the ground and waggles it at me. "It's going to sting you so good, Tatey-Tot."

"Um, thanks?" I take the toy from him when he flops it against my cheek.

"You're welcome. I've got a matching one and I can confirm those bees know what they are doing." Monty winks at me. I find the button on the toy's wide base to turn off the vibrations.

"Yeah, I'm sure they do." I stuff the toy back into the box, then pile the rest of the spilled contents back inside, too.

"That's enough pranks for one day, boy. Why don't you come with me to get the last few boxes from the car before you get yourself in trouble?" Luke steers Monty out the door with a grip on the back of his neck.

"He's rambunctious," Daddy comments, but he's smiling as he watches my bestie leave our apartment while trying to finagle a funishment out of the gag gift.

"Wouldn't have him any other way." I grin at Daddy. "Can't believe we're really doing this." I glance around at the boxes of my things in his space. I thought it might be overwhelming to take this plunge with him. Gary made me doubt my judgment and whether I could rely on any daddy for a long time, but Rory's different. I trust him to treat me as his equal with the big important decisions, so I'm not scared of letting him take the lead on everything else.

"Second thoughts?" he asks, all concern for me as he wraps me in his arms.

"Nope. This is perfect." I mean it, too. Daddy always takes good care of me, and that won't change just because I'm sharing a roof with him.

"Good." He kisses my nose, then turns me toward our room. "Then you might want to put the *actual* sex toys away before Monty gets back to tease you more." He tips his chin toward the box on the couch labeled 'boring adult things'.

I laugh. "You figured out the decoy?"

"I might not know Monty as well as you, but that seems like the last box he'd snoop through." Rory shrugs.

"Yep." I lift the box in question.

"You want to unpack now, or later?"

"There's no rush, right? Can we just hang out and deal with

the unpacking tomorrow?"

"Sounds good to me." Daddy kisses me again. "I love you, precious." His fingers linger on my chin, his lips brush against mine again, tender and sweet.

I moan into his mouth. "Daddy! No teasing." I have to tear myself away to take the sex box into the bedroom before Monty gets back. Daddy swats at my butt playfully as I pass him, but he goes to restack the boxes with my little toys in them next to the already put away toys.

I dump the contents of my box into one of the dresser drawers Daddy cleared out for me. We can sort through my big boy toys after Monty and Luke leave. The two of them get back with the last boxes full of my little gear as I step out of the bedroom. Daddy directs them to our room. Monty looks ready to snoop some more, so I distract him by showing him my new penguin race car.

Monty and I play with my toys in the living room while our daddies make our dinner and get to know each other. When they first got to my place to help with the packing, it was weird to see Luke interact as Monty's daddy. He even had to use his 'Daddy means business' voice when they arrived. Monty got distracted by playing with my toys instead of helping me pack up the last few items.

Luke offered him a spank if he needed help to focus, which made me squirm to think about until they actually did it. Then it wasn't much different from the dozens of times I've watched Monty play in the past. Except that seeing how much Luke settles my bestie helped me push past my initial awkwardness at seeing Luke in action as Monty's daddy. It's obvious that they bring each other joy.

I always want them both comfortable being themselves around me, and that includes Luke offering Monty what he needs. The rest of the day has gone more smoothly with that initial hurdle out of the way.

Even better, Luke is getting along with Rory. The two of them are talking while they fix our food and I catch enough of the conversation to be assured that they're on their way to forging a friendship. Sure, they're comparing notes on daddying Monty and me, but we aren't the only topic of conversation. That seems like a good sign they have more in common than us.

After the initial rush of joy at agreeing to move in with Rory, I thought I might have anxiety about the decision. We'd only just added sex to our relationship, after all. But now that we're sharing that kind of intimacy, I don't want to spend our nights apart. And I trust him. The fact he waited for me for months made it impossible not to trust him. Daddy always puts my needs first. I haven't had any second thoughts about living with him.

I was anxious, though, that my three favorite people wouldn't get along during our first dinner get together. But now that I know they do, my nerves melt away and I can relax into racing with Monty. Playing together with my toys while our daddies socialize in the kitchen is a fantasy the two of us have shared for years. The reality lives up to my expectations.

If someone had told me last spring that missing littles' night at Adventures for a work emergency would lead Monty and me to this moment, I'd have laughed. But it turns out that faulty plumbing led us each to one fateful night and from there, to the perfect daddies for each of us. I smile at the realization that we can both trace our relationships back to that same night.

Rory calls for us to wash up for dinner and Monty turns it into a race. The entire meal is chaotic and fun and delicious. It's a perfect night, surrounded by the people I love. And when Monty and Luke head home, my daddy puts me to bed and makes love to me. It's the perfect way to start our life together.

***

Thanks for reading Service Call! If you enjoyed Tate and Rory's story, please consider leaving a review to help others find them. And be sure to grab a copy of Picture Perfect, Connor and Jax's story at: www.amzn.com/B09YDN81N7

Looking for more stories like this one?

There is a short bonus scene about Tate and Luke's younger years available in my FB group at: https://www.facebook.com/groups/alexsalcove

If you're looking for more Summer of Adventures be sure to check out the rest of the series at: https://www.amazon.com/dp/B09D627KGK

Summer of Adventures is a spin off from my geeky contemporary romance series Table Topped available at: https://www.amazon.com/gp/product/B08R6LM6YG

And if you want more kink from me, check out New Ground, an M/M/X urban fantasy novel with psychic links and daddy kink at: www.amzn.com/B08NHQFJDZ

ABOUT THE AUTHOR

Alex Silver (he/them) grew up mostly in Northern Maine and is now living in Canada with one spouse, two kids, and a lovebird. Alex is a trans guy who started writing fiction as a child and never stopped. Although there were detours through assisting on a farm and being a pharmacist along the way.

Visit me online at:

http://alexsilverauthor.wordpress.com/

Browse my entire book catalog at:

https://www.amazon.com/Alex-Silver/e/B07NPBW615

Join my Facebook group at:

https://www.facebook.com/groups/alexsalcove

Follow me on BookBub at:

https://www.bookbub.com/profile/alex-silver

Follow me on Twitter:

https://twitter.com/asilverauthor

Sign up for my newsletter for a free short story at: https://landing.mailerlite.com/webforms/landing/i2w6l7

And as always, consider leaving a review on Amazon or Goodreads if you enjoyed this book, reviews are of vital importance to independent authors, thanks!

OTHER WORKS BY ALEX SILVER
Summer of Adventures
Kinky Contemporary Romance

Dungeon Master (M/M)
Knotty Boy (M/M)
Service Call (M/M)
Picture Perfect (M/M)
Puppy Love (F/X)
Stud Muffin (M/M/M)

Table Topped
Contemporary Romance

Roll for Initiative (M/M) Book 1
Charisma Check (M/M) Book 2
Saving Throw (M/X) Book 3
Plus One Bonus (M/X) Book 4
Dump Stat (F/F) Book 5
Party of Three (M/M/X) Book 6

Shift Work
Omegaverse MPreg Romance

Papa Bear (M/X)
Squirrel Trouble (M/M) (expanded edition)
Trash Panda (M/M)

Hauntastic Haunts
M/M Paranormal Romance

Dan's Hauntastic Haunts Investigates:
Goodman Dairy (*Book 1*)
Hawk Lake (*Book 2*)

Ivarsson School (*Book 3*)
Joliet Asylum (*Book 4*)

Free download links to the shorts are available in my FB group: https://www.facebook.com/groups/alexsalcove
Drew's Haunted Hangout (*A Hauntastic Haunts Short Story 1*)
Rafael's Haunted Halloween (*A Hauntastic Haunts Short Story 2*)
Lee's Haunted Holiday (*A Hauntastic Haunts Short Story 3*)

Psions of SPIRE
Urban Fantasy

Shelter (M/M) Novella 0.5
Bright Spark (MMMM) Book 1
Bold Move (MMMM) Novella 1.5
Keen Sense (M/M) Book 2
Weak Link (M/M) Novella 2.5
Quick Fire (M/X) Book 3
Clear Sight (M/M) Book 4
New Look (M/M) Novella 4.5

A SPIREverse daddy kink standalone
New Ground (M/M/X)

Shared Universe Series
Super U - Superhero Romance
Super U: Rising Storm (M/X)

Final Days - Zombie Romance
The Willows (M/M GNC)

Anthologies
Listen: The Sound of Fear
Haunt (M/M trans gothic horror)

Fix the World
Upgrade (gay trans cyberpunk)

SUMMER OF ADVENTURES
CHARACTER GUIDE

Martin: Owner of Adventures, MC in Dungeon Master who discovers a kinky boy in the cafe where he's forced to work when his office gets flooded.

Bobby: A barista who first appears in my contemporary series, Table Topped, and finds love with a regular at the cafe where he works. Martin sweeps him off his feet with a whole new world of kink after a misunderstanding about just what sort of dungeon Martin runs draws them together in Dungeon Master.

Monty: One of Connor's closest friends. Tate's best friend. A pudgy boy with ADHD who discovers that his best friend's brother is his perfect Daddy in Knotty Boy.

Luke: Tate's step-brother and Monty's Daddy. He specializes in ropes and suspension bondage and gives workshops on the topic. He and Tate are also business partners. Realizes his brother's best friend is the perfect boy for him in Knotty Boy.

Tate: One of Connor's closest friends. A plumber who owns his own business along with his step-brother, Luke. He is dyslexic and into age play/ABDL. Finds his Daddy after a chance encounter leads to more in Service Call.

Rory: Tate's Daddy. A trans man who moves to Vancouver for his career as a voice actor and rediscovers his kinks as Tate's Daddy. Finds love after a one-night stand in Service Call.

Connor: Quent's best friend. A shy, pierced, Jewish, trans boy looking for his perfect caregiver who can also be his partner. Finds love when his kinky friend with benefits grants all his wishes in Picture Perfect.

Jackson: A kink photographer who offers Connor a kinky friends with benefits relationship the turns into so much more in Picture Perfect.

Quent: Also goes by Q. A fun loving nonbinary pup who uses they/them pronouns. Connor's best friend. They are in a long-term relationship with their Mommy, Kylee. The pair has an ethically nonmonogamous relationship that is open for sex and kink, but closed romantically. Quent and Kylee struggle to deepen their relationship when Quent offers to be a surrogate for their brother in Puppy Love.

Kylee: Quent's Mommy. She is a trans woman who is a motherly figure to all of Quent's little friends, particularly Monty, Tate, and Connor. Her story is told in Puppy Love.

Harry: A contractor who is kink positive. Harry met Quent when he helped with renovating Quent and Kylee's home playroom. He is Connor's friend group's DM for their regular D&D sessions. He also handles the renovations at Adventures for Martin.

Clark: A pup handler who appears in multiple books along with his partner. Niko is his pup and husband. They have an open relationship. His story is coming soon in Stud Muffin.

Niko/Nicholas: Clark's pup. One of the friends pup Q enjoys playing with. He is married to his handler, Clark and dating his boyfriend, Ethan. His story is coming soon in Stud Muffin.

Ethan: Nicholas's boyfriend who sometimes plays with Clark and Niko together. His story is coming soon in Stud Muffin.

Hope: Angel's Domme and partner. They have a teenage daughter, Bethany.

Angel: Hope's sub and one of Luke's go-to rope models for demonstrations and workshops. They are married to Hope and Bethany's parent. The pair appears in several books as members at Adventures.